Sisters in Space

The Complete Series

Adapted from the screenplays
of the seven episode webseries

David R. Beshears

Greybeard Publishing
Washington State

ISBN 978-0-9969077-4-3 *(print edition)*

Greybeard Publishing
P.O. Box 480
McCleary, WA 98557-0480

Sisters in Space

The Complete Series

Adapted from the screenplays
of the seven episode webseries

Episode One

"Awakening"

The universe beyond the forward viewport was jet black and all but featureless. There were only a few very faint stars to indicate the cosmos wasn't totally empty.

Within the shuttle's cockpit, occasional faint beeps and tweets were the only sounds that broke the blanket silence. There was no sound of human activity, no muffled rumble of engines; nothing but the quiet existence of the shuttle's computer system going about its solitary business.

The only illumination came from tiny indicator lights on the front panel set before the view window and those in the console between the two empty seats; that and what little light managed to reach in through the narrow opening leading to the main compartment.

The main compartment was sixteen feet long, lit only by the soft glow of panels set beneath a pair of sleeper canisters that were recessed into the port wall, set behind clear plastic panels. Claire lay in the upper canister, her sister Amelia in the lower. They were dressed in beige cryo-support coveralls, monitoring and bio tubes attached to the synthetic sleeves and at the waist. They lay comfortably asleep on thick cryo-support sleeper pads.

Claire was twenty two years old. She was tall and thin, with a thin face and long, straight brown hair. Amelia was twenty years old, a few inches shorter than her sister. Her hair was wavy and several shades lighter.

Storage compartments were set into the bulkheads to either side of the sleeper canisters. Set into the opposite wall was a computer station, a small kitchen station, food storage and the shuttle's water recycler.

A narrow table was fixed to the floor in the center of the compartment, with small benches attached on either side. A door to the rear of the cabin led to a smaller compartment that held main storage and the sani-closet. Beyond this was the EVA gear room and airlock.

At the rear of the shuttle was the power room. But for the rare course adjustment to avoid one danger or another, the power room had been quiet for a very long time. Once the desired direction and velocity had been attained, there had been no need.

The shuttle traveled silently in the empty black of space, its two occupants unaware of the passage of time, deep in cryo-sleep, fed and cared for by the shuttle's bio-system, their bodies aging at the rate of three minutes with each passing month...

Several alert lights flashed in the cockpit. A series of soft beeping sounds broke the silence and a small, square panel that had lain dormant for years began to glow. Back in the main compartment, the overhead lighting turned on, set to low and providing minimal illumination. The panel below the sleeper canisters came to life and changes were made to the fluids that fed the occupants through the bio tubes.

Adjustments to cabin life support were made in preparation of the awakening passengers.

Once all was ready, each canister's clear wall panel slid aside. A few moments later, Claire opened her eyes, and then Amelia opened hers. They lay unmoving, blinking, staring uncertainly above them.

Amelia, in the lower canister, finally rolled onto her side and sat up, placing her bare feet onto the floor. She took in several long breaths, only then looked about the main compartment. She looked side-glance at a pair of feet that appeared suddenly beside her, attached to legs dangling from the upper canister.

"Is that you, Claire?" she asked dully. Her voice was raspy. She hadn't spoken in she didn't know how long.

"Yeah... me," Claire said casually, her voice just as rough. "Uh... where are we?"

"Looks like a shuttle."

"I see that. I don't remember a shuttle."

Amelia looked back behind her, into the canister. "It's the tube I went to sleep in." She looked again into the shuttle's main compartment. "This is definitely not the transport ship."

Claire slid delicately down from the upper canister, looked about the compartment as she sat beside her sister.

"This looks like a *long recon* shuttle," she said. She looked again side to side. "Small. Two person team."

"Claire? Um... how did we end up in a recon shuttle?" asked Amelia. Not that she expected an answer.

"Something must have happened to the transport. We got moved." Claire continued to study their surroundings. "The others must be in another shuttle."

"I hope so. If something did happen—"

"I'm sure they're fine, Amelia."

"There were over three hundred people on that ship."

"I'm sure they're fine," Claire repeated, this time with a bit less conviction.

They were both quiet then for a long moment, each with their own thoughts.

Uncle Marcus? Danny?

Amelia finally looked forward, in the direction of the cockpit.

"I wonder where we are," she thought aloud.

"Near Trinahr, I imagine," said Claire. "The system woke us up for a reason."

Amelia continued looking in the direction of the cockpit, but made no effort to stand up. "I expect we should find out."

"I expect so," agreed Claire. She also showed no signs of standing.

Amelia looked in the other direction then, gave a half nod and managed to get to her feet.

"Sani-closet first," she said. "I need to get cleaned up."

"Right behind you," said Claire. She watched Amelia stagger awkwardly to the rear of the compartment, and again looked forward. She stood and started toward the cockpit.

Claire slid into the pilot's chair. She took only a moment to look out the forward view window and then tried to ignore the emptiness out there.

It didn't look much like the Trinahri system they had been destined for.

She quickly scanned the various boards on the forward panel and the central console, familiarizing herself with the configuration. She reached out then and confidently touched several pads, flipped a couple of switches. Panels illuminated as the nav system came on line. An eight-inch monitor flickered to life as text and numbers displayed and scrolled.

Claire didn't like what she was reading.

She reached out to her left and ran her fingers across several other touch pads. More panels illuminated and another small monitor came to life.

The ship's autopilot confirmed what the nav system had already told her.

Claire leaned back in the pilot's seat and frowned. She looked more closely at the view outside. She was still staring out the forward view window when Amelia came into the cockpit and settled into the copilot seat. She had changed into work coveralls.

Amelia took in that same view of the outside. "Oh, that can't be good," she said.

"It's not."

"So where are we?"

"A very long way from where we should be."

Amelia was bringing up the ship's main computer on the copilot primary monitor. She stopped and looked over at her sister.

"And where is that?"

Claire sat up, leaned forward and began running her fingers across touch pads. "I don't know."

"Claire? How can you not know?"

Claire continued tapping at a panel. "We are way, way into uncharted space," she said. "I can tell how far we are from where we should be. I can give you the path we've been on. I can tell you how long we've been on that path."

"And?"

"Eighty years."

Amelia turned quickly back to the computer station, began running her fingers across the console.

"That can't be. That can't be."

"Sure it can," Claire stated matter-of-factly. "We've been traveling at ten percent the speed of light for eighty years, fourteen days and a couple of hours; direction consistent at ninety three degrees in the wrong direction, with the rare course adjustment to avoid hazards."

Amelia fumbled with her thoughts. "Okay... okay... so what do we do?"

Claire shrugged a shoulder. "Turn around, start back."

"Another eighty years?"

"What choice do we have, Amelia?"

Amelia leaned back in her seat. She stared out at the black empty space before them. From all she could tell, they could have been sitting motionless in the dark, but Claire had just said they were travelling ten percent the speed of light; in the wrong direction.

"Eighty out, same back. If I'm up on my math, that's one hundred sixty years," she said numbly. "Everything... everyone..."

"We don't know what happened to the others," said Claire. She was working again at one of the panels. "They could be in the same fix we are."

"Come on, Claire. That's a stretch. And that's assuming they even made it off the transport."

"And I'm going to assume that for now." She gave a slight *hmm* sound and frowned at a small screen. "This could be why we were brought out of cryo... the nav array is down."

"A blessing in disguise," sneered Amelia. She nodded sharply at the forward view. "We could still be asleep; another hundred years; a thousand years."

"Even on recycle, cryo tubes don't have supplies for a thousand years, Amelia."

Amelia frowned. "You're not making the situation any easier, Sis."

Claire ignored her, swiped a fingertip across a panel and it went dark. She looked to Amelia, then back behind them, into and beyond the main compartment.

"It's not software," she said calmly. "It's the array itself."

Amelia grew coolly serious. "Can we fix it?"

"Hope so. It's gonna take an EVA."

"Fine. I'll do it."

"No, I'll go. I have more hours, and I know navigation arrays better than you."

They stared at each other a few moments. Amelia finally swiveled her seat about.

"Fine. I'll help you suit up." She started out of the cockpit. "Let's get this over with. I want to get this bucket turned around. Every second puts us further from home."

The gear room was small compared to the main cabin. There were the two suit closets on the right, the access hatch to the airlock on the left. The open area in between was for donning the suits.

Each suit hung on a heavy hook that was set into a ceiling track. Amelia pulled one out from its closet, sliding the hook along the track, as Claire shrugged her way out of her cryo-coveralls. Underneath she wore a two piece base layer covering her from ankles to neck. She had to disconnect several fittings that held the base layer to the coveralls.

She backed into the suit, stepping into it.

Amelia supported her, holding her by the elbows.

"It's going to be clumsy, Claire," she said. "No getting around it."

"I have never liked these one size fits all suits," said Claire. "I know they say it adapts, but it never fits like my own suit."

"Well, we're a long way from our jumper, so think before every move."

"Thank you, Nana."

With all the fittings and seals in place, Amelia brought the helmet from its shelf in the closet and set it into position over Claire's head. She turned it forward and locked it down. She took a toolkit from a drawer in the closet and clipped it to Claire's suit.

"It's the standard kit."

"Got it."

Claire moved over to the airlock hatch, turned to face Amelia so that her sister could activate a panel on the chest plate. After a few moments, Amelia looked directly into Claire's helmet faceplate.

"All good, Claire. You?"

Claire read through the status lines on the internal display within her helmet. She took a moment then to evaluate how everything felt physically.

"Good to go," she said at last, giving her sister a thumbs-up. She faced the airlock's inner hatch and pressed the touchpad beside it. The door opened and she stepped through.

Amelia closed the hatch behind her sister and looked through the porthole. Claire lifted a hand and waved heavy-gloved fingers without turning. She pressed another touchpad and the outer door opened. The black of space lay before her.

She took hold of a D-clamp fastened to one end of a support line and hooked it to her suit. She took the other end and reached outside, found the recessed eyelet on the hull beside the door. Once connected, Claire allowed herself to drift out of the airlock.

Back in the main compartment, Amelia settled in front of the computer station. She pressed a fingertip to a touchpad and the monitor came to life. A few keystrokes on the smooth keyboard panel and she picked up Claire's helmet cam.

"I have your feed, Claire," she said. The tiny mic in the monitor picked up her voice and fed it to her sister's helmet. "How do you read me?"

"I read you just fine, Amelia." From the display, it looked like Claire was already maneuvering into position. "This old bus is really showing its age."

"So I see. Looks like about eighty years of micro-meteors, eh?"

Claire reached a panel cover set into the hull, the short, squat navigation array beside it. "The array looks fine, but take a look at this cover."

There was a deep indentation in the cover, and two sides were bent upward, creating an opening along the exposed seam.

"It took a heck of a hit," said Amelia.

The shifting movements of the image on Amelia's monitor indicated that Claire was studying the damage from different angles, likely looking for a way to get into the nav box.

"The latch is useless," she heard her sister say. "I'll have to pry it open."

"I don't have to tell you to watch yourself, do I?" asked Amelia. "There are some sharp edges on that cover."

"By all means, Amelia. Please do point out the dangers of the vacuum of space."

"Don't get snotty."

Claire's gloved right hand came into view on the monitor. She had a small pry tool in hand. Using it on the panel cover, it took only a few seconds to get it open. The narrow beam of light from Claire's helmet lamp exposed damaged wiring within the small compartment.

Claire sighed. "This is going to take a while."

"Take your time. I'm not going anywhere." Amelia sat back and folded her arms. "I'm not going anywhere at ten percent the speed of light."

Claire stepped down from the cockpit and into the compartment. She was dressed now in the same work coveralls as her sister.

"Course is entered," she said. "System is still calculating burn to turn us around."

"Good, good..." Amelia nodded without looking away from the computer station's monitor. She was tapping at the keyboard panel, her expression alternating between curiosity and frustration.

Claire went to the food storage cabinet, brought out a dry ration packet and sat at the table.

"D'you find anything?" she asked. She opened the packet and began eating the bite-sized food pellets.

"Some," said Amelia. "It looks like there are media files in the log, but half are corrupted and the index is toast. If I can salvage something from the directory, I might be able to bring up one of the less damaged files; at least a piece of one."

"You'll get it," said Claire. "That's what you do."

"Yeah..." Amelia let out a distracted sigh, her focus on the monitor. "We'll see..."

Claire was about to respond to that when she hesitated, leaned forward and turned her head aside. She felt it first, and then heard it; a faint rumbling through the deck plates, through the seat and the table.

The engines were coming to life.

Amelia spoke over her shoulder, still tapping at the keyboard panel and her focus still on the monitor in front of her.

"Sounds like systems finally figured out how to get us home," she said.

"We'll be there before you know it," said Claire. She smiled and tossed another food pellet into her mouth.

There were flashes of light and shadow then from Amelia's monitor, crackling static sounds, and finally broken pieces of words.

Amelia straightened and leaned nearer the console. She brushed her fingertips across the keyboard panel. The monitor display quieted as the sounds went silent.

"Amelia?" Claire prompted, standing and coming around the table. She stood beside her sister.

"Trying. Like I said, these files are—"

"Corrupted, damaged, yeah. I got that."

The screen flickered, images flashed and disappeared; more static noise from the tiny speakers.

The frozen image of a young man flashed onto the screen, his expression as though he had been speaking and was now stuck in mid-word. He was in his early twenties, had light brown hair and a friendly face. From his look, he definitely had something worrisome on his mind.

"Danny..." said Claire, and she shifted position to be a little bit nearer her sister and the monitor. "What does our dear brother have to say?"

"Working on it," said Amelia. She was working intently at the keyboard. The image on the screen vanished and was replaced with a light blue window half-filled with rows of text and code. She brought up several smaller windows and pushed these to one side, continued entering lines and running the code.

"Well?" asked Claire.

"Bits and pieces, at best."

"I'll take whatever we can get."

"That is our only option," Amelia sighed and tapped at several more pads.

The work-windows on the screen dropped away and a new image of their brother Danny popped up. Static noise and broken bits of words crackled through the speakers and Danny's image jumped and started, eventually smoothing out.

"Good morning ladies... so..." Danny hesitated, smiled his familiar thin smile. "Surprise."

"Uh, huh..." Amelia grumbled. Claire just grinned knowingly and shook her head.

Danny's smile faded. "As you may have noticed, you're no longer in the transport. About that... a bit of an incident here, I'm afraid. The Jensauri chose now to break the truce, and they chose an attack on our transport to announce this change in policy. Our luck, eh?"

"Pretty much, yeah," mumbled Amelia.

"Since you're watching this, it means we weren't able to pick you up on the other side. Sorry about that. So, real quick here... not much time. Catch you up as best I can. Things were getting out of hand. The crew woke Marcus, what with Marcus being, *you know,* Marcus."

"Good ole' Uncle Marcus," mumbled Amelia.

The video flickered suddenly and Danny's image jumped and individual words became disconnected from one another. Half a sentence more and the display jumped again, and then again, Danny's face morphing, the audio hissing and sputtering.

"Oh, come on," Claire groaned. "It was just getting interesting."

"Like I said—"

"Yeah, yeah... bits and pieces."

Danny's image solidified but the audio continued to break apart as Danny went on.

" -- took a turn—escape chambers—released—chamber—holding our particular group of sleeper tubes—damaged—tried—not going—" There was a sudden jumble of images, and then Danny's smile froze on the screen. "More—luck—eh?"

"Wouldn't have expected anything less," said Amelia.

"Don't be a party pooper," chided Claire.

The screen display jumped and the audio crackled and hissed. Words broke and whole sentences were lost. After half a dozen frustrating seconds, the picture quieted down and the audio cleared.

"... knew from the shipping manifest that there were four survey shuttles on board. He woke me to help, and we transferred you into one of 'em." Danny glanced aside, gave a nod to someone off camera. He looked again directly at the screen. "I've set a heading for ninety degrees away from all the fun. The plan is to rendezvous with you in thirty days. Alternate meet-up location is a hundred days further out."

Danny's expression grew dark.

"You're watching this, so we missed both rendezvous points. Once again... sorry." He leaned forward, appeared to be keying something in. "So... get this bucket turned about, set a course for Trinahr, and I hope to see you in about seven months."

Seven months... The sleeper tubes had originally been programmed to wake their occupants at seven months, that being the scheduled arrival date of the transport at Trinahr. Claire and Amelia had yet to discover what had gone wrong.

Amelia grumbled, "And it looks like we missed the seven month rendezvous as well."

Danny's face unexpectedly popped out of existence. The screen went blank; the compartment was suddenly very quiet.

Amelia leaned back in her chair, continued staring at the monitor. She said nothing, was frowning.

"All right, then," Claire sighed. She looked down at Amelia. "That explains one or two things. It leaves a few holes, for sure, but gives us more than we had."

Amelia folded her arms across her chest, glanced up at her sister. "It doesn't help us any, though, does it?"

"What's to help?" Claire pushed away from Amelia and started back to the table. "We're already doing what we can; heading home. I'm just glad to know something of how we got here."

Amelia said nothing to that. She stared at the now blank screen, struggling to keep back the anguish.

Claire looked over at her sister. She let out a long breath, looked down then at her hands, fingers intertwining.

"I know, Sis..." she said softly.

Everyone was gone... everyone they ever knew... They were alone...

Claire and Amelia worked over the next several days to make the shuttle ready for the return journey. It had travelled more than eighty years on auto, and while the ship was able to maintain and service many of the systems on its own, there were some things that were better assessed under the human eye and served by the human hand. Over that eighty years, there had been wear and tear.

While Claire was only twenty two years old, she had been qualified to pilot a shuttle for three years, performed frequent maintenance on her family's small jumper and knew it inside and out. This long-range shuttle, while different in some ways, was in most ways very similar. Claire felt absolutely comfortable preparing it for an eighty year return trip. She divided her time between the cockpit and outside running a pair of EVAs. As she had seen on her first EVA, the hull had endured hundreds of micro-meteor hits over the years. The ship's monitoring system hadn't logged any breaches, but a thorough inspection was long overdue.

Amelia meanwhile focused on the ship's computer systems, cryo-canisters and inventory. She had been working computers from the inside out since she was nine. She carried on better relationships with computer AIs than with most humans. Claire was one of the few people she got along with, and she could barely tolerate her.

Returning from her second EVA in two days, Claire stood silent as Amelia helped her out of the suit, a clumsy and awkward affair. She slipped into her coveralls as her sister slid the suit back into its locker.

"All right, Sis... what's up? You're not the bright and chipper Amelia we've all come to know and love." Claire waited expectantly as her sister secured the suit and gear in place. "That's sarcasm, by the way; something you may not be familiar with."

Amelia turned and leaned a shoulder against the wall of the locker, folded her arms and looked down at her sister, who was sitting on the small bench, slipping into her shoes.

"Ship didn't wake us because of a damaged nav system. The logs don't match. Not even close."

Claire stood up. She knew the bad part was yet to come. "Then why?"

"We were running out of time in the cryo-tubes."

Claire knew what that meant. They were a long way out in the middle of nowhere. They were deep in uncharted space and she had no idea where the nearest habitable planet might me.

"How much is left?" she asked simply.

"Maybe thirty months." Amelia pushed off the wall, stood straight. "We have all the ingredients necessary in food inventory to process more of the cryo-juice, but it takes time. And to be honest, even if I used all the rations we have, it'd only give us another forty-eight months."

"You said we had twelve years of rations. All that bubbles down to four years of cryo-juice?"

"Afraid so."

Claire sat silent for a long moment, thinking over all this new info. "Let's hold off on that for now. Twelve years rations with eyes open, and two and a half in cryo. That still leaves a lot of space between us and home."

"Hence my concern," Amelia said coolly.

Claire thought on that. She stood then, sharply.

"And well-founded concern it is, dear sister," she stated decisively. "I'm hungry. How about lunch?"

Amelia watched numbly as Claire walked over to the hatch and stepped through into the main compartment. It took her a few seconds to shake herself out of it and follow her to the main compartment.

She mumbled in disbelief. "Claire? Lunch?"

"Absolutely." Claire pulled a hot-pack out of the food locker, walked over to the warming unit and tossed it in. "And today... I deserve a hot lunch. I worked hard this morning. This old boat is cleared to go."

"But we're not," said Amelia. "We have less than a fifth of the food inventory we need, and that's including the cryo-juice. What do you suggest we do?"

Claire took the short stride to the table and sat on the edge to wait for her food to heat. She looked side-glance at her sister, gave her a gentle smile.

"Listen, Sis. Considering the course we've been on, we can't be more than a few years in uncharted space. Once our nav system can plot our position, we'll set a course for the nearest friendly habitable planet and restock." Claire winked. "No problem."

"Oh, I so wish you hadn't said that. I really don't like when you say that. It never, ever goes well when you say that."

A sharp *ding* sound came from the direction of the food warmer. Claire pushed herself from the table.

"Lunch time."

Claire and Amelia were sitting in the cockpit, each going through last minute checks of all systems. It had taken five and a half days for the ship's nav system to complete the turnaround, but they were finally on course for home.

Claire finished the final checklist of the navigation system. Amelia ran final checks on environmental systems and cryo systems.

The sisters would be going into the tubes for twelve months. It didn't make much sense to run eyes-open while in this featureless void, but they also wanted to keep some months of cryo-juice held in reserve. The compromise was to initially go in for a year, see what things looked like then.

Amelia had set the cryo-tubes to wake them at twelve months, but as a backup had also reset the low-juice alert to bring them up in the event it fell below eighteen months. Both should trigger at about the same time.

They still didn't know why they hadn't been awakened after seven months, which had been the original wake-flag.

"Checklist complete," said Claire. She set her head back against the headrest. "Nothing now but the waiting."

Amelia finished her own checklists. She swiped a fingertip across a touchpad and her monitor went black.

"Right."

"Good." Claire was looking out into the dark. Now that they were turned around, there was a new splash of stars before them. They were still very distant, but at least there were more of them. Not many more, but more. It made it all seem just a bit less ominous.

Amelia leaned back now in her copilot seat. She let out a long breath. She wasn't quite ready to go into cryo.

She looked out at that cluster of stars.

"Sure hope those look closer when we wake up."

"I just hope we wake up," said Claire playfully.

Amelia gave her a look that said *I've done all I can... what more can I do?*

Claire shook her head sadly, gave a sly grin. "Lighten up, Amelia. We'll be fine."

They sat in silence, each lost in their own thoughts, staring out into the empty black.

Amelia looked to her sister, then again forward. "You know, at some point we're going to have to actually leave the cockpit and get into the cryo tubes."

"Mmm. S'pose so."

"Yeah."

There was no rush.

Episode Two

"Out of the Void"

Claire was by herself in the cockpit, unhurriedly going through the nav systems. She hadn't been out of cryo long, was still wearing her cryo-coveralls.

Initial checks didn't reveal the threat of imminent destruction; so far, so good. She next began a run-through of the ship's most recent diagnostics. As she did so, she gave another quick glance out the forward window.

The cluster of stars they had been traveling towards during their time in cryo was closer; still a long way off, but significantly closer. The splash of shiny objects set against the black of space took up more of the view than before, and if one were to hazard a guess one could now point to the one they were heading for.

Her reviews complete, Claire initiated several new diagnostics. With these running, she left the cockpit and stepped down into the shuttle's main compartment. The overhead lights were on. Amelia was still asleep in her lower-berth cryo-tube.

Claire took a ration packet from the food cabinet and sat down at the table. She absently ate from the packet as she just as absently watched her sister's tube come to life. Indicator lights on the cryo-tube board came on; one of them flickered and flashed. There was a change in the background hum as automated adjustments were made to the cryo-juices that were being fed through the feed-lines.

It was another minute before Amelia's berth sidewall slid aside. It was yet another half-minute before Amelia opened her eyes. It took her a while to orient herself to where she was.

She slowly rolled onto her side and sat up. Seeing her sister sitting at the table, munching on ration pellets, she rubbed at her temple and furrowed her brow.

"Claire?"

"Good morning, little sister." Claire tossed another pellet into her mouth.

"Is everything all right?" asked Amelia.

"Right enough."

Amelia was still pulling her thoughts together. "What are you doing up? I mean, we were scheduled to come out of cryo together."

"Yeah. I changed that."

"What do you mean, you *changed that*?"

"I thought I would take a peek first. There was no sense both of us coming up if we had to go right back in."

"That's crazy." Amelia rubbed at her temple again. "And I want to be in on any decisions involving keeping me in cryo."

Claire shrugged, tossed the last ration pellet into her mouth. "You say so."

"I say so." She frowned and stood up. "I need an aspirin."

"Headache? I came out with one too. Better now. What's up with that?"

"I don't know." Amelia went over to the med station and found a sealed packet with two aspirin. She broke the seal and dropped the aspirin into her palm. She tossed them into her mouth and swallowed. "What's our status?"

"I let you come out of cryo, didn't I?"

"Please, Claire..."

"You have so never been a morning person."

Amelia stepped over to the table and sat down opposite Claire. She stared coolly at her sister, said nothing.

"All right, all right," said Claire. "We came out of cryo right on schedule. Twelve months. The ship's systems all look good. I'm running additional di-ogs right now."

"What about our location?"

Claire leaned back. "Yeah... we've made some real progress, but..."

"We're still in the void..." more of a statement than a question.

"Yup," said Claire. "That we are."

Amelia finished wriggling into her work coveralls and then stepped into her shoes. Her morning ritual continuing on schedule, she left the gear room and entered the main compartment. Claire was up in the cockpit, so she had the cabin to herself.

As per the daily routine.

She selected a hot ration packet from the supplies and tossed it into the food warmer. She had one hot meal each day, and she usually chose breakfast. She felt it gave her the best start to the day.

This was day ten since coming out of cryo. Each day was pretty much the same.

Actually, after the first day, each day was <u>exactly</u> the same.

On the first day they had run complete systems checks and inventories. After that, it was all rather routine; monitoring, mostly.

The shuttle travelled. They were in a void. Empty space. Not much to do.

They had enough rations to last them twelve years. That sounded like a lot, but they had initially travelled in cryo for eighty years. They were only one year into the return trip. They would need to restock if they intended to get all the way home.

When they had last gone into cryo, there had been thirty months of juice in the system. Inventorying after coming out of cryo, they had about eighteen months remaining; close to what they had expected. This meant, however, that without resupplying, they would have to use cryo very sparingly.

And that meant that they would, at least for the time being, ride this time in the void with eyes open.

Amelia could only hope it wouldn't drive her stark-raving mad.

She brought her hot breakfast ration to the table and sat down. She ate alone, in silence, with only the never-changing background white-noise of the ship going about its own daily routine.

Up in the cockpit, Claire sat staring out the forward view window. She had finished the morning checks, found nothing that needed following up on. The ship was pretty good at taking care of the routine operations, and most of the conventional issues that arose as well. It could even work its way through many of the unanticipated problems that came up.

Those issues that needed human hand and eye turned out to be rare, especially out here in the void.

Claire twisted about in the pilot's seat and glanced back through the open door to the main compartment.

Maybe Amelia was up for another game of cards.

Day sixteen since coming out of cryo. Amelia had been sitting at the computer station in the main compartment all morning. Claire was at the table playing solitaire. She glanced up occasionally and looked over at her sister.

Amelia could be a bit of a bore sometimes. A couple of hundred card games and all of a sudden she doesn't want to play anymore.

Claire put the black seven on the red eight.

Amelia tapped at the keyboard panel, hesitated, tapped again. She stopped, studied the monitor. She sat back, frowned at the screen.

"Hey, Claire?"

"Yeah?" Claire droned. This time she didn't bother looking up from the cards on the table.

"You should come look at this." Amelia didn't look away from the monitor.

"Why?" Claire placed the red six on the black seven.

"Really. Come look at this."

Claire set her cards down and stood up, stepped around the table and looked over her sister's shoulder at the monitor. "What am I looking at?"

"Text file."

"I see that. What is it?" Claire read for a moment. "Oh.... from Danny?"

"Sent to us a week after we left the transport." Amelia looked up at her sister. "I was just doing some house cleaning, found this. I wasn't even in the mail folders, wasn't in the comm system at all."

"So rather than a mail packet, he sends us a cryptic text file and dumps it into an obscure folder."

"It was a folder he could get access to." Amelia looked back at the screen. "It's not that cryptic."

Claire gave a soft *hmmph* sound, then she read aloud: *"Things are looking rather hectic here. Best you postpone your visit."*

Amelia nodded slowly. "I would say that was pretty clear, Claire."

Claire grumbled to herself, folded her arms and looked sharply at the screen, as if it might reveal something more. It didn't.

"At least we know that Danny was alive a week after he packed us into this shuttle and sent us out here to... wherever *this* is."

"And it might explain why they missed all of our rendezvous points."

One of the overhead light panels flickered several times and there was a *beep-beep-beep* alert from the direction of the cockpit.

Something was up...

Claire headed forward without saying another word. Amelia followed after her, settled into the copilot's seat and watched her sister bring up the nav system.

After another half a minute, Claire still hadn't said anything.

"Well?" asked Amelia.

"Ship's eyes finally see something out there. There's some data coming in."

"And?"

Claire made a face and shrugged. There wasn't much. Not yet. A few preliminary calculations on time estimates to the nearest bodies. There was no data yet on the planets or the stars themselves. To the positive, this was the first sign of the edge of the void.

"Still a ways off," she sighed. "Three weeks, maybe."

"I can do that," said Amelia. "Having any target data at all helps."

So true, thought Claire.

And they would soon start getting more data on the nearer planets. More info would give them more options. They weren't alone out here in the empty black anymore. They wouldn't just be heading for the nearest white speck in the night. They would soon be able to pick a planet and go there.

Amelia dragged herself into the cockpit, still half-asleep, still dressed in night-clothes. She was holding a mug of hot liquid breakfast with both hands. She settled into the copilot seat and looked groggily across at Claire.

Claire had been awake for more than an hour, was showered and dressed, and had finished her breakfast. Her attention was on one of the monitors. She spoke without looking at Amelia. "You look awful."

"Good," said Amelia. "I'd hate to think I felt this bad and it didn't show."

"If you didn't spend half the night on the computer and went to bed at a decent hour—"

"What's the good news, Claire?" asked Amelia, cutting her off.

Claire tapped several keys on one of her control panels and jerked her head toward one of Amelia's monitors. Amelia swung around and leaned a few inches in the general direction of the screen her sister had sent data to.

"Hmm. Pretty," she said.

"That's the system we're approaching," said Claire. "If we stayed on course, that's where we would be in another eight days."

"And by that you mean we are not going to be staying on course."

"There's nothing there for us."

It did, however, together with a number of other systems and stars that were now within range, give them enough nav data to calculate where they were in relation to charted space.

Claire shifted to her left, tapped a few more keys, and another system showed on Amelia's screen. "This is where we're going, just as soon as I finish adjusting our course."

Amelia studied her screen. After a few moments, she separated one of her hands from her mug and tapped at her keypad. The diagram zoomed out, showed the target system in relation to the shuttle's location. Data appeared on a second monitor.

"Twelve days." Amelia was starting to wake up now.

"Janus Two."

"I don't think I've heard of it."

Claire gave a sly grin. "Second planet in the Janus system."

"Most helpful, Claire."

"It was originally a remote supply outpost, edge of charted space; established in the earliest days of the expansion. Long-since outgrown its status as an outpost, now a colony of 20,000."

"So we should be able to replenish supplies."

"That's the plan," said Claire. "I don't know about cryo-juice, but certainly rations. And maybe we can replace some equipment that's on its last life."

Amelia raised a brow. "And news? Maybe find out what happened? I know they're a heck of a long way out here, but after eighty years, ya' gotta figure even they should know something."

Claire turned back to her nav station. "For us, even old news would be news."

"Yeah." Amelia frowned and took a drink of her breakfast. "Their lag time must make communications just about useless."

"And they're not exactly on regular shipping lanes."

They must have traveled within shouting distance of the Janus system on their way out of charted space and into the void.

The two fell into a casual back-and-forth as Claire continued prepping for the course change. At this point the conversation was mostly to fill the silence. Amelia didn't mind silence, preferred it in fact, but Claire hated it.

"All right," Claire tapped a last key, shifted around and faced her sister. "New course is laid in, Janus Two in twelve days, give or take. Plenty of time for you to take a shower, eh?"

The data coming in regarding the system they were approaching became more detailed with each passing day, as well as expanding the data of the sector as a whole. The ship had chart and navigational data in its database, but specific information regarding each of the five planets, assorted moons and other bodies was very limited and outdated.

As they drew nearer the Janus system, Claire and Amelia had expected to start receiving the normal indicators of an inhabited planet. A long-standing population of 20,000 made a lot of noise and displayed a significant footprint. There should be radio, broadcast, and other communications bleeding out into space. And the ship's sensors should also be receiving the environmental evidence of a large colony. It should be shining like a beacon to the stars.

They weren't picking up any of that. Claire and Amelia were growing anxious. All was not right on Janus Two.

Two days out, Amelia began attempting to make contact with the colony, sending messages every two hours. There was no response to communications.

One day out, still no indicators, and still no response to communications. They were, however, now close enough that they were able to identify a ship in orbit.

"Larger than a shuttle, smaller than a transport," said Amelia. She was reading the data coming in on one of the copilot consoles; row after row of scrolling text.

Claire was reading her own set of data. Her nav system was just able to pick up the object in orbit. They would be maneuvering into orbit themselves in another seven hours. "I'm not reading any activity," she said. "I think it's a derelict."

Nothing from the surface, and an abandoned ship in orbit... not good.

Amelia slid back in her seat, dropped her head back and looked out the forward viewport at the distant planet.

"I don't think there's anybody home."

Claire put the shuttle into a high orbit above the planet. There was still no communication from the surface, and there were still none of the expected indicators on the shuttle's sensors.

Amelia fed the system sensor processes and communications to the computer station in the main compartment and left the cockpit. She felt more comfortable in the main cabin. She filled a water bottle from the dispenser and settled in at the computer.

Claire came down from the cockpit a few minutes later. She sat at the table, arms and elbows on the tabletop, facing her sister, frowning, studying the back of Amelia's head.

"Could they be playing dead?" she asked. "Maybe they're hiding from whatever happened."

"I don't think so," said Amelia. "True, there's no sign that anything bad has happened, other than there's no sign of life, but... I mean there is *absolutely no sign of life*. If there was anybody down there, hiding or not, sensors would have picked up something. I'm getting nothing. They're not there."

Claire tried to think of some other logical explanation. "Right," she said at last. "But we still need supplies."

"I don't think we should go down there," said Amelia. "Something bad <u>did</u> happen. They either all left, or they all... *you know*. Either way, the bad may still be there."

"Hmm." Claire stood behind Amelia. She studied the data currently displayed on the monitor. "The derelict," she said.

"Excuse me?"

"We'll dock with the derelict. There may be supplies aboard, and we may find out what happened."

"And if whatever happened on the surface is also on the ship?"

"We'll suit up. That should protect us." She placed an open palm on her stomach. "But first... lunch."

§

Claire's experience with docking was mostly with the family's small flyer. But she had qualified as part of her training, and the truth was that the shuttle would do most of the work. So long as Claire didn't put the operation into full-manual, the ship's systems wouldn't let her do anything that would do any serious harm.

Nonetheless, once Claire had guided the shuttle into the docking path with the derelict and they had closed to within a thousand yards, Amelia climbed out of the copilot's seat and started out of the cockpit.

"I'm going to go prep the suits."

"You're a snot," said Claire. But she managed a grin. "Fine. Go. Big sister will take care of everything."

"Uh, huh," and Amelia was through the access and into the main compartment.

Claire continued monitoring the docking procedure. Fortunately the ship they were closing in on had the standard docking hatch, so once within range the shuttle sent and received back the appropriate signal and locked in the approach. A few moments later the shuttle slowed to maneuvering speed.

The shuttle moved in beneath the ship, slowing further to docking speed. There was an adjustment as the shuttle stopped its forward momentum and glided upward. There was a gentle thump and bump; Claire heard and felt the clamping system link the two ships together.

By the time Claire got to the gear room, Amelia was into her suit. Claire slipped out of her coveralls and climbed into her own suit. They both then began putting on their gloves.

"I don't like this," said Claire, for the second time. "One of us really should stay in the shuttle."

"Too bad. If anything happens, I'd just as soon we were together."

"Fine." Claire handed Amelia her helmet, grabbed her own and lifted it over her head, slipped it on and locked it into place.

They checked each other's fittings, checked gauges.

Claire activated her suit's communications. "You're good," she said. "How do you read?"

"Read you A-Okay," answered Amelia. "You're good to go."

They worked their way into the airlock and sealed it. This was a vertical docking, and the round docking hatch was overhead. Claire activated the panel set beside the ladder and checked to verify the connection was still good. She activated the hatch and it opened inward.

The connecting hatch had to be opened manually. Claire climbed onto the second rung of the ladder and took hold of the bar handle. She twisted it a quarter turn left and felt it lock into place. She then turned the latch and pushed the hatch inward.

She and Amelia climbed up into the corresponding airlock and closed the hatch behind them.

The ship was ten times the size of their little long-range shuttle, but the individual rooms and compartments they passed as they headed forward weren't much larger than their own main cabin. Reaching the bridge, Amelia settled into one station as Claire sat at the station beside her.

After half a minute the emergency lighting came on, a number of system panels activated; the bridge glowed soft amber.

"Thank you, Sis," said Claire as she went to work.

"My pleasure," Amelia answered absently. She continued tapping at the glowing panels in front of her.

"Restoring environmental systems now," said Claire. The systems and interfaces were all pretty standard, the ship looked to have been around way back in Claire's time, and for some time before that.

As Claire continued to wake up the ship, Amelia began searching logs and communications. "There's not much in crew logs," she said. "Maybe there's something in the system logs."

"Communications?" Claire was still working on the environment systems.

"Last comm was eighteen years ago. Same for system logs. Give me a minute to see what's in them."

"Environment approaching normal," said Claire. She studied a stream of data. "There's nothing nasty in the air."

Despite that observation, neither made the move to take off their helmets. Claire kept monitoring the waking environment systems.

Amelia continued to study system logs. "There's nothing out of the ordinary in the system logs going back thirty days prior to what looks to have been a standard system shutdown."

"They were in orbit that whole time?"

"It looks that way." Amelia shrugged. "Then they just turned everything off and left."

"Boarded a transport?"

Another shrug from Amelia. She looked closely then at communications. There was nothing of content saved, she was only able to see a history log of communications to and from the ship: when, how long and addresses. In the month prior to the ship systems shutdown, there were several dozen outgoing communications directed to a single station on the planet at regularly scheduled intervals, each lasting from one to three minutes.

There were just two incoming communications in all that time; one three days prior to systems shutdown, the other two days prior to systems shutdown. They came from a single source, each lasting under half a minute.

Claire pushed back from the station and stood up.

"Where are you going?" asked Amelia.

"To see if I can find anything on a walk-through. You keep digging. There has to be something."

"I should go with you."

"I'll search the ship, you keep doing what you're doing." Claire left the bridge and started back along the central gangway.

The commons was a combination rec room, mess and living area. It looked to have been little used in the days leading up to the ship being abandoned. There were two empty mugs sitting on a table in the far corner of the room; nothing else.

After checking stores, good news there, she continued her search. Crews' quarters looked neat and tidy. A few odds and ends left in drawers, nothing mounted on the walls. Passenger compartments were just as sparse.

She found her way finally into the short, wide hall containing the set of pod rooms; four compartments each containing twelve cryo tubes. The containers in the first three compartments were empty, as was to be expected. The ship had been powered down, after all.

Walking into the fourth compartment, she came to a lurching stop in the middle of the room. For several moments she wasn't able to do anything more than stare blankly ahead.

Two of the tubes in the far wall were occupied. The glow of the overhead light panels shone on the clear front panes of the containers and on the bodies within.

They had been dead for a long time; that much was obvious. But she couldn't understand how that could be. All ship's systems had been completely shut down, and that wasn't possible with active cryo tubes. The ship wouldn't allow it.

Not unless there had been intentional tampering.

Suicide? Go to sleep and never wake up? There were worse ways to go, Claire supposed.

She stepped nearer the occupied cryo containers; a middle-aged man in the upper berth, a woman in the lower. They could have been a couple. Likely were.

What could have driven them to this?

Amelia looked up from the console as Claire came back onto the bridge.

"There you are," she said. She gave a slight nod at the monitor. "From what I can tell, the ship went on auto shutdown. I don't think there was anyone on board at the time."

"I see," said Claire. She walked slowly over to the next station and sat down.

"Pretty standard mothballing procedure," said Amelia. "I did come across a single personal log entry. Found it on an independent station, not in the main archive. I think someone on board was communicating with family on the planet."

"Really?" That caught Claire's attention.

"Which would explain the regular comm status records listed in the history log."

"What did it say? The personal entry, I mean."

"It was a final message, a last goodbye. Just a few words, but without the context, it's rather cryptic. I think they had already said goodbye, this was something different. They were reaching out... one final time. I think they wanted to leave something behind, just in case."

Claire said nothing at first, barely acknowledged that she had heard. Finally then, hardly above a whisper, "Sounds about right."

Amelia gave her sister a curious look, but let the odd comment go. "So what'd you find?" she asked. "Anything?"

Claire came out of her reverie. "The good news, they didn't take everything with them when they left. There's a store full of rations. And water. We won't be relying just on re-cyc anymore."

"Thank goodness. What about cryo-juice? I couldn't bring it up in inventory."

"That's the bad news."

"No cryo?"

"No cryo."

Amelia let out a glum sigh. "Ah. Well... so we're traveling eyes-open for a while."

And they would be traveling eyes-open in their own shuttle. Even if they'd wanted to switch ships, the derelict would never be in any condition to leave orbit.

They were each suddenly lost in thought, each drawn to very different images drifting across their mental landscape. Amelia slowly stood up then.

"What say we get those supplies transferred over and get out of here?"

"Sounds good to me," said Claire. "The sooner we're off this boat, the better."

Claire left Amelia in their shuttle's main cabin and stepped up into the cockpit. She spent several minutes entering their departure sequence into the ship's nav system. She hesitated a moment then, and initiated the procedure.

The docking clamps disengaged. Once confirmed, small jets fired and the shuttle pushed slowly away from the larger ship. Some seconds later, once at a safe distance, larger thrusters fired and the shuttle began to move quickly from the derelict. Claire verified their status, initiated the sequence to take them out of orbit.

Returning to the main cabin, she found Amelia sitting at the table. She had a bottle of water in front of her, was absently staring at it.

Claire sat down opposite. "We're on our way."

Amelia nodded; she lifted the water bottle in toast and took a drink. "Non-recyc," she said. Her mind was definitely somewhere far, far away.

"Are you all right?"

"Sure," said Amelia. "I'm just fine."

"Great," grumbled Claire. "Kind of hard to tell, you know. Your 'all right' aura and your 'not all right' aura are pretty much the same aura."

Amelia couldn't help but grin at that. She tried not to, but it showed up on her face in spite of herself.

"Sorry."

"Yeah," said Claire. She pointed to the bottle of water. "How's it taste?"

"Good. Real good." Amelia took another drink. She looked up from the bottle then, looked at her sister. "Are you going to tell me about the dead couple that you found in cryo?"

"Ah. So you know about them. System logs? I was planning on telling you."

"Two cryo tubes were taken out of the system ahead of the shutdown, but remained online. Only one explanation I can think of."

"Me, too."

Both had pretty much come to the same conclusion. By intent or by misfortune, someone had been left down on the planet. When everyone else aboard the derelict transferred to another ship and left orbit, the two found in the cryo tubes had been unwilling to leave those down on the planet behind. At some point months later, following their goodbyes, the two had tampered with the ship's systems, put the ship into auto shutdown, and had gone into cryo sleep. When the cryo-tubes depleted, there would have been nothing to wake them up.

Claire and Amelia still didn't know the reason for the planet being abandoned. It may or may not have been related to what had happened to them eighty years earlier; which they had yet to fully understand.

Amelia turned her attention back to the bottle of water.

"Eight weeks, huh?"

"Give or take a couple of days," said Claire. They were headed for a colony twelve times the size of the colony on Janus Two. "We might run into something sooner. Data on this region of space is both sparse and old."

"Eight weeks," sighed Amelia.

"Give or take."

"Uh, huh..."

"Hey," Claire perked up. "I brought some games over from the derelict. I know you're tired of cards... I found a dice game; and checkers... you wanna play checkers?"

Episode Three

"Ghost Ship"

Claire had come up with what she thought to be one of her best games yet. It was a little bit handball, a little bit table tennis.

The unique component was deactivating the gravity plating.

Amelia hovered near the aft end of the main cabin, Claire forward near the access to the cockpit, with the table between them in the center of the room. The idea was to hit the small rubber ball back and forth to one another using their bare hands, with the requirement that the ball had to bounce off the top of the table with each pass.

It was the lack of gravity that made the play interesting.

Amelia pushed off to the left, reached out and swatted at the ball. The ball headed forward toward the table as Amelia continued traveling in the direction of the cryo beds. She twisted slowly about and her shoulder hit the upper berth panel.

Meanwhile, the ball bounced softly off the table and continued toward Claire. Claire drifted to her left and swatted the ball. It was a hard, downward stroke. The reaction of the ball, however, was an easy arc back to the table. It drifted up and glided aft to the rear hatch.

Claire let out a cheer.

Amelia held onto the cryo bed panel, hovering a foot above the deck.

"I'm done, Claire." She wasn't enjoying the game quite as much as her sister.

"Come on, Amelia," said Claire. "You're doing great. You're only down by three."

Amelia shrugged her shoulder as she rubbed at the spot she was certain was going to bruise. She had already expressed her concern that one of them was going to break something, but that had fallen on deaf ears. No use bringing that up again.

"I prefer my sports in one G," she said instead. "Less chance I'll bring up my lunch."

A low tone alarm began to sound, reaching into the main compartment from the cockpit. One of the overhead light panels flashed.

Claire and Amelia exchanged curious looks.

The signal meant that the ship's sensors were picking up something; which they shouldn't. There was nothing out there.

Claire turned about and pulled herself forward through the hatch and into the cockpit. Amelia had a more difficult time, clumsily pushing and pulling her way forward. Her arm struck the door jamb of the hatch as she entered the cockpit. She grabbed hold of the back of the copilot seat.

"It's a ship," Claire said to her absently.

"Anyone we know?" Amelia worked her way around and pulled herself down into her seat. She locked her feet into the toe holds.

Claire ignored the sarcasm. "It's not moving."

"Not another derelict."

"Don't know yet."

"How far away?"

"Six hours, current speed." Claire was already running the calculations to slow the shuttle down. They were traveling ten percent light speed, and the sequence to park the shuttle alongside the ship was going to be rushed. If they weren't going to fly right past it, they would need to start slowing down immediately.

"We should have seen it a lot sooner," said Amelia. "Why didn't we see it sooner?"

"I don't know. Initiating deceleration sequence." Claire ran her fingers across one of her panels. "We'll come up alongside it in... just under twenty hours."

"All right..." Amelia gave her sister an exaggerated smirk. "Can I have my gravity back, now?"

§

Amelia stepped up into the cockpit, two cups of coffee in hand. She handed one to her sister as she sat in the copilot's seat. She looked out the forward view window.

They had slowed to approach speed and were continuing to slow as they drew nearer the ship.

It was twice the size of the last derelict they had come across, was big when compared to their own shuttle, but was still quite small by most measures. There was no landing bay; the only access was the docking hatch.

As they continued to approach, they saw signs of external damage. There was an open wound in the hull; a blackened tear running along the starboard side.

The tear ran right across the docking hatch.

It appeared as though the hatch was open. To either side of it, the skin of the hull was torn and pulled up.

"We won't be docking," said Claire. "We'll never get a lock."

"So what do we do?" asked Amelia.

"I'm not sure."

"One of us needs to go over there," said Amelia.

"I agree." Claire shifted position and began working at a console. "I'll get us close. You make the hop-skip-jump over, see what's what."

"Really? I mean, I thought you'd fight me on this."

"Like you said, one of us has to go."

"Yes, but I was sure you'd want to do it."

Claire wouldn't look at her sister. She continued working at the console set to her left.

"I do. But I have to stay here. I'm a better pilot." She hesitated. "Now go suit up."

Amelia finished running the self-checks on her suit, these all the more critical without Claire there to do the buddy-check.

"Ready," she said, reaching out and opening the airlock.

"Helmet cam, please," came over the helmet intercom.

Amelia reached up and tapped a button on her helmet.

"Thank you," said Claire.

"You're welcome." Amelia closed the airlock door behind her, stepped forward and opened the main outer hatch.

They were alongside the other ship. It was now only a few dozen yards away and was moving steadily closer. The docking hatch was directly across the open space.

The hatch door itself was gone, sections of the outer hull's skin to either side of the opening torn and jagged.

"Whatever happened, it couldn't have been pleasant," said Amelia.

"Hear that," said Claire.

Amelia attached a safety line to her suit, then to the recessed eyelet to the left of the hatch. The two ships drew a little closer, then held steady at thirty feet.

"I don't dare get any closer," said Claire.

"It'll do."

Amelia aimed and gently pushed off, the safety line trailing behind her.

Claire watched the crossing on the monitor set into the forward console, the video feed coming from Amelia's helmet cam. The damaged hatch access came up quick, and she didn't like the look of the torn metal. It wouldn't take much to damage her sister's suit.

She said nothing. The danger was obvious and she didn't need to tell Amelia to stay away from sharp objects.

There was a slight jarring of the image as Amelia landed at the access and stepped awkwardly into the airlock. The gravity plating was active. That was good news.

"The inner airlock hatch is open," said Amelia. She disconnected the safety line from her suit and let it drift, then moved through and into the ship's interior.

"Can you close it?" asked Claire.

"I'm trying now."

Claire could just see the panel that Amelia was working with, her helmet lamp providing what light there was. It looked like most of the ship's lights were out, though from the shadows that Claire had seen there had to be some emergency lighting.

"Nothing," said Amelia. It could have been damage to the door itself or to the operating mechanism. The power to the airlock door was independent of other systems.

Amelia left the gear room and entered the central passage. She started forward, and after traveling twenty feet she came to an open hatchway. She had to lower her head and lift her feet to step through.

"That's an interior bulkhead, Amelia," said Claire. "Can you close the hatch?"

Amelia said nothing, but the image on the monitor spun about as she turned around. While the hatch could be closed remotely under power, Amelia was able to manually push it closed on her own. When she lowered the bar handle, a small light above the hatch lit up.

"Positive lock," said Amelia. She turned and continued forward. "I'll find a console, see if I can get environmental systems up."

Claire relaxed just a little. If Amelia could get environment up and running, she would be significantly safer. The cold vacuum of space was a very dangerous place, even with a suit and helmet.

Claire watched Amelia's advance along the passageway on her monitor. There were only a handful of small emergency lights, these set far apart and creating a dull grayish glow in the corridor. A beam of light from Amelia's helmet lamp reached out ahead and stabbed and slashed into the gray.

Those tiny emergency lamps had no doubt been dimly lighting the way for years. Claire thought it made the scene lonely and sad.

She saw a shadow flitter across the passageway some way up ahead of Amelia. It had no form, really, was a misty shadow among darker shadows.

And then it was gone.

Claire studied the monitor, afraid to blink, afraid she would miss it should it appear again.

"Amelia, did you see that?"

The steady march up the passageway appeared to slow.

"See what?" asked Amelia.

And then, again on the monitor... another apparition drifted across the passageway up ahead of Amelia. It passed from an open door on the left to another directly opposite. And then it was gone.

The scene on the monitor froze as Amelia stopped in her tracks.

"Oh, geez..." mumbled Amelia.

"That," said Claire.

Claire stared at the monitor, her mind momentarily numb.

Blank. The screen was blank. The monitor had just gone... dead. Live feed, and then nothing.

She stabbed at the interface reset pad. Nothing happened. She tapped again, repeatedly, calling out to her sister. Only then did she realize that the audio had gone dead as well as video.

But that didn't make any sense. Amelia's helmet cam and the audio intercom were on separate and isolated systems.

Okay, okay... keep it together... no good if you freak out...

Claire leaned forward and worked anxiously at the keyboard panel, trying desperately to reestablish one or the other, audio or video.

She heard something. A crackling, hissing white noise came through her headset.

"Amelia? Amelia? You there?"

"Yeah, I'm here," said Amelia. She sounded calm; almost overly so.

"Amelia?"

"I said I'm here. What's up?"

"I lost you," said Claire, doing her best to bring it all back down. *Don't freak your sister. Don't freak your sister.*

"Lost me?" Amelia sounded more curious than concerned.

"Sight and sound. Both went poof."

"Poof?"

"Yes. Poof. Still no video. Are you all right?" Claire was quickly regaining some semblance of calm.

"I'm fine." And she sounded fine.

The monitor flickered back to life as Claire continued tapping at the keyboard panel. She lifted her fingers and leaned back. It wasn't due to anything that she had done. It was just back.

The image was of the passageway, a closed hatch now only a few yards ahead.

"You're back," she said, as calmly as she could.

"Good to hear," said Amelia. "I missed me."

"Not at all funny, Amelia." Claire hoped her grin didn't come across in her voice. "So what happened?"

"Nothing happened. I don't know what happened."

"Well, don't do it again."

"I'll try." Amelia was again moving down the passage. "It could be interference from damaged systems that are still live."

"After all these years? How can anything be live?" There were the handful of emergency lights scattered about the ship, but that network was designed to last like... indefinitely.

"I know, but... Claire, I don't really know how, but it doesn't look like years."

"What do you mean by that?"

"I don't know. I mean... it just doesn't look like it's been years."

The display on the monitor spun slowly about as Amelia turned her head and looked back behind her. Another shadow moved into the passage ten feet further down the hall, drifted toward her and then disappeared through another doorway.

Claire felt a prickly chill pass through her. Those shadowy specters on the monitor were beginning to take on more solid form.

"They're human," she whispered, loud enough that the intercom picked it up.

Amelia faced forward again and continued up the passage.

"I don't think they can see me," she said. "At least not yet."

"What?" *What the heck did she mean by 'not yet'?*

"They seem to be busy going about whatever it is they need to be going about doing."

The display on the monitor flickered, went static with white noise and then as quickly cleared.

"Hey!" Claire called out without thinking.

Amelia came to a sudden stop. "What?"

"Don't you go dark on me again," said Claire. She suddenly felt foolish.

"What?"

"The video. It... never mind."

"Uh... okay." Amelia was on the move again.

"Just... I don't want you disappearing on me. If we lose contact, I'm bringing the shuttle in and I want you to head back to the airlock."

"Okay," Amelia said again. "Understood."

"Good. Good."

Claire watched as Amelia reached the forward hatch. She opened it, stepped through and entered the ship's bridge.

There were shadowy specters everywhere, all seemingly quite busy and none taking notice of Amelia.

Claire watched the monitor as her sister's helmet cam took her slowly across the bridge, amongst and through the specters and toward a console inset along the right wall. The shadowy figures looked to be taking on more solid form by the second. And they appeared to be moving about with purpose, just as Amelia had said earlier.

Once at the console, Amelia began making awkward swipes across the panel with her gloved hand. The helmet cam also picked up shadowy movements reflected off the plastic surface of the console.

"All environmental systems coming online," said Amelia.

"The ship's power plant quietly waited for you to come along and wake it up?"

"I'm not so sure it was asleep," Amelia said quietly. She was still thinking that all wasn't as it seemed.

Claire said nothing, watched as Amelia brought other systems displays up on the console one by one, activating some, letting others remain offline.

Something must have caught Amelia's attention, because the image on the monitor suddenly shifted up and out across the bridge.

Figures were in position before several of the consoles; some of the specters were obviously standing, others apparently sitting. The forms shimmered, drifted in and out of focus. From what Claire could make out, they did indeed appear to be very busy going about their business, and were for the moment ignoring Amelia.

The focus of the display swung back around and returned to the console.

"Environmental readings all show green," said Amelia.

Claire saw Amelia's gloved hand as it passed briefly across the screen. "What are you doing, Sis?"

Amelia unlocked her visor and raised it to the open position. After a moment then: "Cold. Breathable."

"Don't take off the helmet," said Claire. If anything bad happened, Amelia needed to be able to quickly seal the suit. Besides, the helmet was where the camera was located.

"I wasn't planning on it," said Amelia. The display on the monitor shifted dizzily and then Amelia started across the bridge. "Time to do a little more exploring. I want to check out supply."

Amelia wanted to see if inventory matched what she had seen online. She stepped through the hatch and into the main passageway.

What Claire saw through the helmet cam surprised her. The damage in the long hallway was much worse than when her sister had passed through just a few minutes earlier. Walls had buckled, several ceiling panels hung askew, and the lighting, which had previously been off, was now flickering on and off. A thin cloud of smoke was drifting out of one of the open doors.

"Geez!" Claire blurted, then quickly, "Sorry."

"Hey, I get it."

"What the heck's going on, Amelia?"

"I'm getting an inkling of an idea."

At that moment a spectral form appeared midway along the passageway, a nearly fully formed human figure. It turned and started toward Amelia, then rushed towards her. Amelia thought at first that he had seen her and was actually coming at her, seeking to confront this intruder. And then she realized, somehow knew, that he was in a hurry to get to the bridge.

Specter or no, Amelia quickly made to step aside to let it pass, but it came upon her so fast that she wasn't in time. The shadow ran right through her.

And she felt it. It pushed through her, pressed at her, tickled at her brain and chilled her deep into her bones.

And then it was past her and behind her and on its way to the bridge.

Amelia stumbled into the small mess hall, made her way to the nearest table and dropped down into a chair; not the easiest thing to do in an EVA suit. While flexible, the suits were still cumbersome and the process of sitting was a multi-step affair.

She heard her sister over the helmet's intercom. The words were soft-spoken, for a change.

"Amelia? Are you all right?"

"I'll have to get back to you on that."

"Why? What's wrong?"

"Nothing. I'm fine."

Amelia looked around the mess as best she could without twisting about in her chair. Furniture was in disarray, the ceiling in the far corner had partially collapsed, and the wall between the mess and the galley looked as though it had started to buckle.

"It's getting worse," said Claire. "How can it be getting worse?"

Amelia didn't respond; she was still thinking it all through.

"Amelia?" Claire urged.

"Yeah?"

"Just checking."

"I'm fine. Really."

"Okay, good," Claire said flatly. She hesitated then. She had been working on an idea. "So, I think I know why we didn't see the ship sooner. You know, not till we were like almost up on it."

"Six hours out," said Amelia. "Before slowdown."

"Right. Whatever. I'm thinking we didn't see it before then because it wasn't here before then." Claire hesitated again, waiting for her little sister the brainiac to break out laughing or otherwise express her disdain. Amelia did neither, so she went on. "It's a reflection. The way I see it, whatever happened to that ship years ago threw this reflection of it into the future, to us; to now. And now, now I think it's being pulled back."

Amelia held her silence. For Claire, that was worse than outright verbal rejection.

"Amelia?"

"Yeah?"

"Well?"

"I believe you're almost right."

"Really?"

"Yes. I agree. I think something bad happened years ago and the ship was thrown into the future, to our present. But it's not being pulled back. The past is catching up."

"Really?" Claire asked again. Amelia almost agreed with her? That was as weird as the idea that she had come up with.

"The evidence points to it," said Amelia. "We are witnessing what happened back then."

"And now that past is catching up to the ship that was thrown our way?"

"And catching up fast."

There was a very long moment of silence.

"Amelia," Claire said at last. "What happens when it finishes catching up to us?"

"I don't know."

"You need to get out of there."

Amelia had the helmet visor down and locked into place as she worked her way aft. She was heading for the airlock, though she had a stop she needed to make along the way. She turned into a side passage and then another.

"Amelia," said Claire, the hint of accusation. "What are you doing?"

Amelia didn't answer.

"No side trips, Amelia."

An explosion... silent at first, distant... and then immediate and powerful. It reached out from the past and sent shockwaves into the present. Amelia was thrown against the wall, went down onto one knee before recovering. She got back to her feet, supporting herself with one hand.

The hatch ahead had closed automatically, blocking her path. Amelia stepped up to it and looked through the window set into the hatch.

The entire section beyond the hatch was exposed to space. Debris was drifting in the black and was continuing to spread.

Claire called to her sister. "Amelia?"

"I'm okay."

"Amelia, I don't think the ship made it. When the past catches up—"

"I'm getting that."

"No more fooling around. Get out of there."

Amelia was already on the move. She had turned back and had started again down the main passageway. There was another side passage that would take her to cryo-juice distribution.

A specter stepped out through one of the doors ahead on the right. The woman was more than shadow, almost though not yet completely solid. She had a bloody gash on her forehead and was holding an injured arm tight to her chest. She was looking directly at Amelia; not past her, not through her, but directly at her.

She sees me...

Was Amelia a shadow to her? A ghost? A specter?

The woman's mouth was moving. She was talking to her, she was saying something but Amelia's helmet audio couldn't pick it up. Amelia and the woman weren't yet in the same time. A few seconds apart? Less?

The woman's expression changed abruptly. She had been surprised by something.

And then she began to drift up from the floor. She held out her one good arm and tried to gain some balance, her hand first on the wall, then up to the ceiling. Regaining a measure of equilibrium, she drifted across the passageway and entered the cabin opposite.

They lost their gravity plating, thought Amelia. *Okay, this is starting to get serious.*

"Their gravity plating went dark," said Claire. "Are you feeling it?"

"This suit is as heavy as ever," said Amelia. *How long do I have?*

The image on Claire's monitor showed that Amelia was on the move, quickly now. She was still traveling the main passageway.

"They can't be more than a few seconds behind us now," said Claire. "That woman saw you."

The image on the monitor began to drift, to swim and rise and fall.

Amelia was now in zero gravity.

The past was quickly becoming the present.

"I'm coming in," Claire called out. "You get to the airlock <u>now</u>."

Claire turned to the navigation console and swept a finger across the screen, began tapping at the key panel. The shuttle shifted slightly, began a slow, controlled drift toward the larger ship. She continued to make adjustments, the shuttle's airlock hatch nudging nearer and nearer the damaged hatch of the ghost ship.

A sudden change in scenery on the monitor that was displaying Amelia's helmet cam image caught Claire's attention.

Amelia had taken another detour.

"Amelia! What are you doing?"

"Cryo-juice."

"What?"

"I saw it in the inventory."

"You don't have time."

"Yes I do. We need this."

"We'll make do without it. Airlock. Now."

"We'll make do better with it."

The cryo-juice closet opened off the general supply room, shared a wall with the cryo chamber. Amelia drifted across supply, held onto a vertical support bar and opened the door.

The walls to either side were lined with shelves, and the shelves were filled with three-foot long lightweight plastic canisters, all interconnected by a network of tubes that eventually fed the cryo beds in the next room.

"Got 'em," said Amelia.

"Yeah? Great... now what are you gonna do?"

Amelia would have to close the valve on each canister, disconnect the tubes and then somehow transfer the canisters from the distribution closet to the airlock and then across to their shuttle.

She drifted into the closet and held onto the right shelf. She closed the valve on one of the canisters, disconnected the tube. She did the same to the next, and then the next. She reached a hand out to the fourth...

A massive explosion rocked the ship. She was thrown forward against the shelf and then back toward the opposite shelf. She felt her helmet strike the shelf, a jolting impact... but it didn't bounce back. It kept going. Her helmet, her body, she was passing through the shelves, the canisters, and the wall behind them. They didn't exist, and yet she could see them, could see inside them, through them.

Claire saw the explosion first on her navigation monitor, then watched through the forward window. It was silent, blindingly bright and all-consuming. It filled all of space.

And then it was gone. Just... gone. There, and then not there. The ship, the destruction, all vanished in much less than the blink of an eye.

Claire had a moment of absolute sheer panic. Amelia! And then she saw her. Amelia was floating, drifting... there, where the ship had been, her white EVA suit set against the backdrop of the black of space.

Claire sat back with a heavy sigh.

Serve you right if I left you out there...

She hesitated, frowned, finally turned again to her navigation console.

§

Amelia finished slipping into her coveralls, fastened the front and then sat down on the bench to put on her shoes. Beside her, Claire was sliding the suit along the ceiling track back into its closet.

Claire hadn't said much since helping Amelia into the airlock and then the gear room; a quiet word here and there, only what was needed to assist her sister out of the suit.

Claire stepped around Amelia and went to the forward hatch, opened it and left the gear room. Amelia finished slipping into her shoes, hesitated and finally stood up. She hesitated again, followed her sister forward through the shuttle to the main compartment.

Claire was standing in front of the food warmer. She was holding two mugs. She held one out to Amelia, then took the two steps to the table and sat down. She took a sip of the coffee, peered over the mug and watched Amelia sit down opposite.

"The ship went back," she stated matter-of-factly. "In the end, when it exploded, it went back."

Amelia nodded. "I figure whatever generated that final explosion is what threw it forward, to our present, and is also what pulled it back to its own time."

Claire took another swallow of her coffee. "Wow."

"At the instant of the explosion, in their time, the ship was sent forward. From our perspective, it came to us in a steady stream. For them, it—"

"It all happened in an instant."

"I think so." Amelia took her first swallow of her coffee. "I felt it, Claire. I felt it leave us. I felt it go back. I was there. I walked the passageways. I activated the ship's systems, breathed in the air. I saw the crew. They saw me."

Amelia set her mug onto the table. She stared at it for a long time. Her breath came in a shudder.

"I felt them drawn back, pulled back, to their time... to their... end."

Claire reached out and took hold of Amelia's arm. "We're going to figure this out, Sis. We're going to figure out what happened to them; what happened to everyone."

"That won't do them much good."

"No, it won't. But maybe we can help make things right."

Amelia had to give her sister a smile. Leave it to Claire. Two young women in a tiny shuttle decades out in the middle of nowhere, decades after whatever it was that happened, and they were going to set things right.

"Well," Amelia said softly. She looked up at Claire, nodded in the direction of the cockpit. "Guess you should get us out of here then, huh?"

Episode Four

"Adrift"

Claire stepped groggily into the cockpit still wearing her cryo-coveralls. She dropped into her seat and swung herself around, reached out and began working the panels, mostly by instinct. She was at it for several minutes before her sister entered and sat down in the copilot's seat beside her.

"We were asleep for 84 days," said Amelia. "We have about 15 months cryo-juice left in the tanks." They had gone into cryo three weeks after entering into this latest void. They had expected to be brought up after 13 months with 5 months of juice remaining.

"The ship didn't bring us out because of the juice," said Claire.

"And that's never a good thing."

"It hasn't been yet."

Amelia was looking through the forward viewport. There was nothing to see out there. "Still," she said. "Out of cryo ten months early is better than out eighty years late."

"I'm not so sure about that," said Claire. She slid back in her seat. "No engines."

Amelia turned sharply to look at her sister. "Waddya mean, no engines?"

"I mean just that. No engines. Ship needed to make a course adjustment, but couldn't activate engines. No thruster jets." Claire raised a brow as she watched Amelia absorbing what this meant.

Amelia turned forward again and again looked out the viewport. She stared at the black.

"So we just coast at ten percent the speed of light until we run into something," she said.

"Which, by the oddest of coincidences, is the very reason the ship needs to make a course adjustment."

§

Amelia lifted the access panel that was set into the gear room floor, slid around and wormed her way down into the power closet. The small room was five feet by five feet. Once inside, she faced the equipment wall. Floor to low ceiling, it was divided into six distinct panels, one above the other. Each panel had its own set of buttons, switches and indicator lights.

At the moment, only two of the panels showed signs of life, their tiny bulbs glowing faintly.

She activated the small intercom on her left. "Mostly dark, as we feared," she said, reached up to the top panel. She took hold of the pair of handles and pulled out the rack. It locked into position before her at a 45 degree angle, exposing the panel box's internals. She brought a diagnostic pad up from her equipment belt and slipped it into a slot behind the panel front cover.

"Hmm... okay," she mumbled.

"What's up?" she heard over the speaker.

"It's not talking. I'm going to have to do this manually." She had half-expected this and had brought a computer interface with her. She unfolded it and set it on the rack in front of her. It had a small keypad and screen.

"Let's do this quickly, Amelia," said Claire. Her voice sounded tinny over the intercom speaker.

"That I shall, sister." Amelia plugged the interface into the panel and went to work.

In the cockpit, Claire was working at the nav station, interfacing with several different databases.

According to every calculation, there were no mapped or documented dangers anywhere along their current course between where they were and their programmed destination. Yet the ship had clearly identified something out there, something in their direct path that required a significant course correction.

Before heading down to the power closet, Amelia had worked her own computer systems outside of the nav system and verified that the reason for the course correction came from something that the ship had seen in their path, and not due to information in their databases. Whatever the ship was seeing wasn't documented.

And based on the calculated course correction, whatever ship was seeing was big.

One of Claire's primary monitors came alive, the screen filling with data. She reached out and swept a finger across a panel, slowing the display. She studied the rows of data, the fonts in white and yellow and blue.

"Hey Amelia," she said, the hint of growing anxiety. "Speed it up, please."

"I'm on it, Claire."

"No... really."

"What is it?"

"We finally have data coming in on what's out there. Half a million miles across, and goes on like forever."

"So, not a planet then." Amelia's voice sounded way too snarky so far as Claire was concerned.

"No," Claire stated flatly. "Not a planet."

"Asteroid belt? Undocumented?"

Claire was studying the data very carefully. "Similar indicators... but I don't think so."

"Why not?"

"The data coming in is wrong." Claire was frowning at the screen. The data didn't make sense. Claire ran it through several diagnostics, but the results were all the more confusing.

The screen flickered and flashed as a new set of data began to feed.

"Oh, boy," said Claire, hardly a whisper.

Amelia hadn't heard her. She had completed diagnostics on half the systems. "Nothing wrong with the systems themselves," she said.

"There better be," said Claire. "And you better fix it. Like, right now."

Amelia hesitated, an oppressive silence. "What is it, Claire?"

"Ships. Hundreds of 'em. Thousands."

"An armada?"

Now it was Claire who hesitated. She was staring at the monitor. Looking up at the forward viewport then, there was still nothing visible.

"Graveyard," she said at last.

"What?"

"A graveyard. We got dead ships coming up fast."

"How fast?"

"You gotta give me something. Real soon."

Back in the power closet, Amelia was on her knees with the bottom panel pulled out and the interior exposed. Several indicator lights were blinking.

"I can give you reverse thrusters," she said.

"We can't maneuver with reverse thrusters."

"But you can slow us down." Amelia had her hands in the panel's guts.

Up in the cockpit, Claire shifted position and began working at her helm board.

"Reverse thrusters responding." Claire looked forward. "This is going to take a while."

Claire stepped down from the cockpit and into the main compartment, dressed now in her standard coveralls. She looked over at her sister Amelia as she went to the water dispenser.

"Where are my engines, Amelia?" asked Claire.

Amelia was hovering over the keypad in front of the computer station. Four hours had gone by, and other than getting cleaned up and changed, neither had taken a break.

"Stapled to the hull." Amelia leaned back, away from the computer, turned about and looked at her sister. "How are we looking?"

"I disengaged reverse thrusters five minutes ago. We're coasting in slow; at current speed, about two hours to the first ships." Claire stepped over to the table and sat down, water glass in hand. "Are you finding anything?"

"The engines are fine, engineering control systems are fine."

"So far, so good."

"My thoughts exactly. I'm thinking maybe something hiccupped in the main computer system itself."

"And computer systems is what you do."

"I can usually find my way around, but not really." *And engines, not so much.*

"So it's fixable," urged Claire.

"Probably."

Claire lifted her glass, realized it was empty and stood up and walked over to fill it. "How do we have thrusters when engines are down?"

"Reverse thrusters are outside of the engine systems. Simple jets, straightforward control box, separate power control."

Amelia heard a short, sharp beep from behind her. She turned slowly about to face the computer station. There was an unfamiliar display was on the screen.

"Well, that's new." She leaned forward and started tapping at the keypad.

"That's no proximity alert," said Claire. It didn't sound anything like the proximity alarm. And besides, they were still hours out and the ship was already monitoring every object out there.

"No, it's not," said Amelia. "We're getting a signal."

"From the graveyard? From one of the ships?"

It took Amelia a few more seconds. "It looks that way. I think there's a message behind it."

"Voice or text?"

"I don't know yet." Amelia was leaning close to the monitor, working at the keypad. "Standard channel, automated signal. Our approach must have triggered it."

"And the originators are probably long gone," said Claire. "Can you retrieve the message?"

"I'm trying to now."

Claire stood beside her, arms folded across her chest, frowning down at the monitor as Amelia brought up and as quickly wiped lines of text from the screen. "Probably a warning; stay away, bad things here..."

"No doubt," said Amelia. *If you're reading this, you're already doomed.* She kept at the keypad, finally gave a sharp nod.

Claire caught the gesture and turned to look directly at the monitor. "You got it?"

"I got it. Video." Amelia checked the file; clean, standard delivery, nothing untoward about it. She attempted to open it. A screen full of gibberish splashed onto the monitor. "Hmm."

"What, hmm?" asked Claire.

Amelia was working at the keypad again. "It doesn't figure. It's a standard video message on an open channel." She finally waved a hand at the monitor. "Everything looks good, but all I get is... *this*."

Claire gave a grunt, retrieved her water and started up into the cockpit. "A dire warning it might be, but right now we could really use engines. I would suggest that this wait until we have engines."

Claire and Amelia were both in the cockpit, monitoring their passage through the graveyard via ship's systems, both with an eye to the forward viewport. At the moment there was nothing to see, but the nav and tracking displays were alive with activity; thousands of dead ships drifting in space, some no more than three or four hundred miles apart. Four hundred miles was nothing in space. The graveyard was dangerously crowded with floating hulks.

"There," Claire stated. She was reading the nav monitor. "Six hundred miles, twenty degrees to port."

"Got it," said Amelia, monitoring her own tracking system display. She lifted her gaze to the viewport, looking ahead and just to the left. Nothing at first... then finally, "There it is."

She was looking at a gray dot in the distance, set against the black backdrop. It was several minutes then before it began to take on form, growing slowly and steadily larger.

"It's big," said Claire. She was still watching the details displaying on her monitor.

Amelia leaned forward slightly, unconsciously, as if those extra few inches would help; she watched the ship draw nearer. It took on the shape of a long, rectangular box, a pair of power nacelles mounted on the top and three landing bays protruding from one side. It was still and lifeless.

"It's a cruise liner," she said.

They both watched through the viewport as it passed on their left, barely a mile to port. Amelia slid back in her seat only after they were well past the ship.

"That was way too close."

"Two more on the way," said Claire, again focused on the nav monitor. "One to port, the other to starboard."

Amelia studied her own display. Eleven hundred miles ahead; it looked like they were headed right between them.

And then the numbers on her screen started changing, driving the real-time running calculations crazy. "Do you see that?" she asked.

"One of 'em is moving," said Claire. "Slow drift. I think we'll be all right."

Reaching the pair of ships several minutes later, they could see that the small ship coming up on their right was in a slow-motion tumble, drifting slowly in their direction but well to their right. There was a shadowy smudge on the hull, starboard side, far aft.

"I think that's blast damage," said Amelia, though at this distance it was impossible to tell for certain.

Hours passed as the shuttle worked its way unguided through the graveyard. They passed dozens, hundreds of ships. Some came near enough to see detail; portholes and landing bays, antennae, identifying markings. A few showed signs of having been attacked. Most were simply abandoned; dark and lifeless.

One of Claire's side panels flickered and scrolled text. She mumbled something to herself, swept a finger across the panel and then activated another process. She turned back to nav control and brought up another display, scrolled and swept aside text.

Amelia watched it all in silence. She knew what it meant. She returned finally to her own systems, sought the ship that the shuttle had flagged and was tracking.

"Oh, boy..." she mumbled.

"Yeah," said Claire.

They were heading directly into the path of a wandering ship. All calculations put them on a collision course. The dead ship and their shuttle would be arriving at the same spot in space at exactly the same time.

"Twenty minutes," said Amelia.

Claire shifted to helm. "Bringing reverse thrusters back online."

"Any slower, we may as well get out and walk."

"We only need a few seconds and the ship will pass ahead of us."

Claire activated reverse thrusters, watched her monitors as the tracking system continually recalculated both ships' courses.

She shut down reverse thrusters. Their speed had dropped another ten percent. She watched the monitors as Amelia searched through the forward viewport. Calculations showed the approaching ship was now on track to pass ahead of them.

"I think we're good," said Claire.

"Here it comes," said Amelia.

The ship was of a configuration they had never seen before. It was large and boxy, had the appearance of rooms being haphazardly added onto it over the years. It had also been damaged a number of times, perhaps from striking other dead ships as it wandered the graveyard.

It passed slowly in front of them, near enough that they could see the seams of the hull plating on the side facing them. It continued its course to their right, and only moments later they crossed its path and were safely past.

Amelia and Claire both slid back into their seats. Claire immediately returned to their nav and tracking systems. Amelia let out a sigh, glanced at her monitors once and then stared out the viewport.

"Okay. So... we're barely moving."

"And we're not crashing into anything." Claire studied her displays. "We're clear for awhile."

"It'll take years to get out of here."

"Not if you fix the engines."

"Ah. Yes." Amelia stood up and started out of the cockpit. "I'm on it."

§

Claire sat alone in the cockpit. The lights were off, there was only the faint shimmer of two of the small monitors in front of her, these splashing an eerie glow onto her face.

She was looking out the forward viewport. Out there, in the dark, were dozens of ships, some drifting, some slowly tumbling, most floating dead in space. Some showed signs of damage, most did not.

The shuttle traveled silently through the graveyard, passing the long-abandoned ships. Claire kept one eye on the monitors, watching the calculations scrolling across the screens, as she watched the ghostly images beyond the viewport.

The shuttle's tracking system indicated that they should pass safely through this crowded sector of the graveyard, but that could change at any time. It would only take one of those drifting ships to bump into another for both ships to change trajectories and for one of them to cross paths with the shuttle. If this happened, Claire had to be ready to kick in the reverse thrusters and hopefully slow them down enough for the untoward ship to pass safely by.

Amelia was sitting at the computer station in the shuttle's main compartment, where she had been working for hours, working her way through the ship's computer systems, trying to discover the reason behind the failure of the engines, barely understanding half of what she was digging through.

She did know that the problem was not in the power control system; nor was it in the main systems, the brains of the ship.

The problem was in the interface, the connectivity between the two systems. She just hadn't as yet been able to track down exactly what that problem was. More confusing still, the ship's ongoing running diagnostics hadn't even seen a problem.

Amelia didn't know enough about the shuttle's complex computer systems, nor how they operated and interacted with one another, to figure out what was going on... or *not* going on.

Claire stepped down from the cockpit and into the cabin just as Amelia growled to herself and leaned back from the console.

"Amelia?" asked Claire.

"Nothing," sighed Amelia. "Frustration."

"Ah. I know it well."

Amelia turned about and looked up at her sister. "I take it we're clear."

"For the time being." Claire sat on the corner of the table, put her feet up onto the chair.

Amelia turned a few more degrees to look directly at Claire. She told her what she knew for certain, as in, what *wasn't* wrong, and then what she suspected, that the issue was somewhere in the interface.

"So, what's the connectivity?" asked Claire. "Are we talking physical lines? Can we replace 'em? Why didn't the ship's systems see the problem?"

"It's a series of comm utilities; system software. And I don't know why diagnostics doesn't see it."

"Maybe it does see it, but doesn't see it as being a problem."

"Possible; which in itself is a problem," said Amelia. She looked at her sister a moment more, then slowly turned about in her chair. She came full circle, again faced Claire. "In any case, the brains and the engines aren't speaking to one another."

"Eighty years without so much as a break, who's to blame 'em?" Claire frowned, slid off the table and dropped into the chair. "So, options... can we shut everything down and reset? Clean the decks?"

Amelia again spun her chair slowly about, speaking softly as she turned full circle. "Not a bad idea, really. Computer systems do get cluttered with time. Maintenance systems are supposed to take care of housecleaning, but from what I can see, I don't think it's happening like it should."

"Maintenance itself needs a bit of housecleaning; brush away the cobwebs."

"Maybe," Amelia said doubtfully.

"Um... one question, Amelia. Shutting everything down... what if everything doesn't come back up?"

"We won't be shutting down environmental systems. They're isolated from the other systems. But I'll be careful. Honest."

"I'd appreciate that."

"This was your idea."

"Now you're just making me nervous."

Early morning; Claire was alone in the cockpit, gazing out beyond the viewport. She was lost in thought and wasn't really looking at anything.

This little diversion was going to make their situation a bit difficult. Adrift, traveling dead slow for days, and once they got their engines back it would take time to get back up to optimum speed. If her rough calculations were any indicator, they were going to need some luck.

They would definitely be digging deep into their stores.

Amelia came into the cockpit, two mugs in hand. She handed one to Claire as she sat in the copilot seat, mumbling a barely intelligible "'morning."

Claire took a sip of her tea. "Thanks. You look like you could use both of these."

"This is my second." Amelia had spent the evening prepping for the shutdown / reboot, and had gone to bed with her mind still diligently at it. She hadn't gotten much sleep.

Claire stared down into her mug. "This is going to work, right?"

"I don't know," said Amelia. "I can guarantee we won't be any worse off than we are now."

"So, the atmosphere won't get sucked out of the cabin."

"The atmosphere will not get sucked out of the cabin."

They sat in the silence then. The dark beyond the viewport seemed to reach into the cockpit.

Amelia looked to Claire, an eyebrow raised. *You ready?*

Claire lifted her mug in toast. *Let's do it...*

With that, Amelia turned to a side panel on her right. She typed at the keypad with her free hand, her other hand holding her mug to her cheek. The small display flashed and scrolled. She held a finger above a key; a slight hesitation. Without saying another word, she pressed the key.

She leaned back, turned forward and took another sip of her tea. Monitors and panels began to go dark, one after the other. The cockpit grew steadily darker until there was only the one small overhead light panel glowing.

Claire gave an anxious survey about the cockpit. *Air?* She couldn't tell. She glanced at one of the narrow air vents. *Was there air coming through?* She resisted reaching up to it.

The last of the systems went down. The shuttle was quiet. They never really noticed how much background noise there was. Now... the silence was shrill against the ears.

Five seconds... ten seconds...

"We're coming back, right?" asked Claire.

"A few more seconds."

A few more seconds passed. Even Amelia started to get nervous.

Finally then, one of the monitors flickered and came to life. A few moments later, a line of text displayed... then several more lines and the screen began to scroll.

A second monitor awoke; moments later, another. Amelia's attention moved quickly from display to display. Steadily increasing white background noise slowly pushed out the silence.

"Initialization diagnostics running on each system as it comes up," she said.

Systems continued to come alive, each running through startup diagnostics before going online. Over in the pilot's seat, Claire leaned to her right, glanced at one and then another monitor.

"Di-ogs are finding a few things."

"Sweeping the floors wasn't enough," said Amelia. "Repair processes initiating."

They watched as several displays stopped scrolling; status lines posted every few seconds as diagnostic programs monitored repair subroutines. One by one then, repairs completed and the systems continued their boot-up.

"All systems read green," said Amelia.

"They all read green before." Claire spoke as she turned to helm and navigation. "Helm likes me."

Amelia had slid forward and was systematically verifying all systems. She continued to work with one hand, not yet ready to set aside her mug.

Claire grumbled to herself. She tapped at a keypad, grumbled and swept a finger across a second panel.

"Helm responds, but engines are still quiet," she said. She brought up another monitor, tapped half a dozen keys, waited, gave a slight *hmmph* sound.

"What is it?" asked Amelia.

"Helm is up and active, but one of those initialization di-ogs of yours is still running in the background; I think it's kicked in a couple of repair processes. Knowing what we know, I'd say when helm tried knocking on the engine room door, it couldn't find it; sent out a repair crew."

"That might take awhile. I need more tea," said Amelia. She swung her seat around and stood up. "All other systems are good."

Claire called over her shoulder to her sister's receding figure.

"Systems up doesn't do us a lot of good if I can't steer this boat. To do that, I need power. I want engines."

Amelia stood in the middle of the main cabin, holding her mug in both hands. There was really no hurry to return to the cockpit. Systems were all back online, Claire was monitoring the repair processes of the interface applications. They would know soon enough if they had their engines back, and in the meantime there was nothing she could do about it.

She took a sip of her tea, looked over the rim of her mug at the computer station.

There was still the matter of the message. She had never been able to get it out of her head. There was something odd about it. Standard message, open channel... sure, there were things that could go wrong over time, but this just didn't look right. The gibberish that came in place of the video feed... it wasn't what she would have expected if the message had been corrupted at the source, or if there had been a problem with the feed.

There was a faint, dull rumbling that she felt rather than heard. It came up through her feet. After a few moments it faded into the background, was gone then unless she consciously reached out to feel and hear it.

The engines were back.

All was well. Claire would once again be tolerable.

Amelia took another sip of tea, looked again in the general direction of the computer station.

Suddenly then... *what if it wasn't a general distress call or a warning?* What if it was a message directed specifically to them? What if somehow, someone knew they would be coming this way?

Danny...

And then Amelia realized why the message, standard and on an open channel, had been garbled. It hadn't been corrupted. The envelope packet containing the vid was encrypted after all, was made to look unencrypted but corrupted.

Danny had wrapped it in code that only his sisters would understand.

Amelia quickly worked her way around the table and sat at the console. She pulled out the keypad and began working just as Claire stomped into the cabin from the cockpit.

"We're good to go, Amelia."

"Yeah, yeah..." Amelia ignored her sister; her attention went from monitor to keypad to monitor.

"D'you hear me? We have engines. We're moving."

"Got it, yeah," Amelia mumbled distractedly.

Claire was baffled.

How can Amelia not be totally psyched?

"What are you doing?" she asked.

"Message," said Amelia, too focused to be drawn away from the flickering of the monitor. "It's from Danny."

"What? How can—"

"Remember the cipher?"

"What?" repeated Claire. "Of course. D-C-A. About as unbreakable as a glass of orange juice." As kids, they had created a childish code they used to encrypt messages to one another. They called it D-C-A, for Danny, Claire and Amelia.

"The message we're getting isn't corrupted. The packet is wrapped in an encrypted envelope, meant to look corrupted."

"But how can it be from—"

"Got it," said Amelia. She leaned back her chair, folded her arms confidently across her chest. The monitor in front of her flickered from lines of text to an image of Danny.

"Surprise," said Danny.

"Geez," said Claire. She moved around to stand beside Amelia.

"If you're seeing this," the recorded video message continued, "then I'm guessing you're Claire and Amelia. So... hello there, Claire and Amelia."

"Hello," droned Claire.

"We tracked your shuttle's path from our last observation, figured you'd be coming by here on your way back. Man, you are really way the heck out there, huh?"

"Bit of an understatement," grumbled Amelia.

"So anyway, we knew this parking lot was here, had a pretty good idea you'd want to be awake traveling through it, and that you'd be slowing down some. A parking lot is as good a spot as any to park a probe with a message for you to pick up." Danny grinned. "Smart, eh?"

"Brilliant," said Claire tiredly.

Danny looked serious now. "A lot has happened since we last spoke; some things you need to know."

Amelia tilted her head slightly and looked up to Claire. "I don't remember him telling us a whole lot the last time, do you?"

"Vague is the word I would use."

"I wish I could say that things are getting better, but... not so much. Maybe a little, around the edges." Danny frowned, his expression grew thoughtful. "Turns out, it wasn't the Jensauri, by the way. Surprise, surprise, we've joined forces. Happened not long after each side realized the other side wasn't the bad guy. The bad guys call themselves the Takiree. Not from around here; I mean, they are like from seriously far away. And the most humbling factoid of all? They're not actually at war with us. They're at war with some other really bad guys back in their home neighborhood.

"Now you're asking, so what's our part in all this?" continued Danny. "I'll tell ya'. We're a resource in their little squabble. We're being conscripted. Collected, shrink-wrapped and shipped off to the other side of the galaxy to fight in their war."

Danny's face contorted slightly and he made a mental shrug. "That, at least, is the latest rumor. No one's actually been there and come back. This is coming from a few folks who've managed to escape the Takiree before they were vacuum-sealed."

"Always one with a pleasant turn of phrase," said Amelia.

"But enough of that," said Danny. "By the time you see this, a lot will have changed, including the facts. I just thought it best you not be completely in the dark as you make your way back. '*Beyond there be dragons*', as they say. Best you know there are in fact dragons.

"And speaking of lizards, Planet X should be your next vacation destination. It comes highly recommended by those in the *comprendo*."

"In the comp—" started Claire, grimacing.

"Counting the days till we see each other again." Danny's somber expression froze on the screen, and then it was gone. Claire and Amelia stared at the blank monitor for several seconds.

"Danny looked older," said Claire finally.

"Some," said Amelia. "Not enough."

"Waddya mean?"

"The date stamp. The message was created just over thirty one years ago."

"Right. We've been *on vacation* almost three times that. He's aged what? Maybe ten years?"

"So he's spent quite a bit of time in cryo."

Claire frowned again and nodded toward the blank monitor. "I don't see why that was encrypted. Nothing to hide, except the coded Planet X reference."

"I don't think it was encrypted for the content," said Amelia. "He didn't want anyone to know we were out here. Better a corrupted distress call than an open letter to Amelia and Claire."

"Right. Makes sense," said Claire, nodding slowly. "So... you gonna make sense of Planet X, decode and point us to where he wants us to go?"

"Danny had to do some painful twisting to get to *lizards*. That and X, I should be able to figure it out."

Claire and Amelia sat quietly looking out the forward viewport. Amelia rested her head on the back of the seat, her hands wrapped around her mug, which she held close to her chest. Several of the forward monitors were active.

The last of the derelict ships showed up first on the monitors. Amelia glanced once at the display, looked out again beyond the viewport. It was several minutes more before they were able to see it; a tiny speck of gray against the black.

Another cruise liner. It passed far to their left. Still, lifeless... empty.

The last of the graveyard ships. Ahead of them now lay only darkness.

Amelia waited, looked over then at Claire. Claire hadn't moved. She continued to gaze out the viewport.

"We can go now," said Amelia.

Claire gave a slight nod, nothing more.

"You okay?"

Claire nodded again, slowly. *All those empty ships... all those people...*

"I'm fine," she said. Claire straightened, leaned forward, absently reached out to the nav keypad.

"Next stop, Planet X."

Episode Five

"Planet X"

They were midway into their fourth orbit of Planet X. From the data coming in, Claire and Amelia knew the conditions on the surface were survivable if not particularly pleasant. The air was breathable, if barely; nothing toxic, but there wasn't a whole lot down there to generate much oxygen. Vegetation was sparse, water more so. It was an arid world with a thin atmosphere.

The planet was slightly smaller than Earth. It circled a star slightly larger but slightly cooler than the sun, though the orbit was somewhat closer. With that, and the rotation and axial tilt of the planet, and the makeup of the atmosphere and landscape of the surface, the days were hot and the nights were bitterly cold.

"I don't care," said Claire. "We're landing."

Amelia shrugged. Of course they were landing. "Just be sure to put us down close to the pod."

"But not too close," said Claire. "I haven't walked twenty feet in a straight line in ninety years. I'd like a chance to stretch my legs."

They had been able to locate the pod easily enough. It was the size of a shuttle and was about the only thing on the planet that wasn't sand, rock or scrubby shrub.

As to the contents of the pod... they had no idea. Danny had sent it halfway across the quadrant, to this specific planet, and hadn't given them a clue as to what was inside. All they had was their brother's cryptic message telling them that they needed to visit Planet X.

Amelia was standing in the cockpit, one hand resting on the back of Claire's pilot seat. The image of the planet below filled the forward viewport, mostly shades of brown and gray.

She slowly shook her head. "Not the most inviting of worlds."

"Probably why Danny chose it," said Claire. She reached out and swiped a fingertip across one of the keypads in front of her. The monitor came to life. "Strap in, Sis, we're going down."

The scene beyond the viewport shifted from that of the planet to the black blanket of space as Claire adjusted their inclination and guided the shuttle into lower orbit. Descending then into the upper atmosphere, the view changed from black to gray. There was a slight buffeting as the ceramic shield covering the bottom of the shuttle began to heat up.

Claire and Amelia were all business now. Bringing a shuttle into a planet's atmosphere was serious, and not something either of them did very often. Both knew what needed doing, however, and both went about getting it done.

Amelia felt a change in weight and pressure as the craft's gravity plating deactivated. She absently checked her safety harness, but her focus was on their descent and their position in relation to the location of the pod.

Claire was silent. She was monitoring the trajectory of the descent, letting the ship's systems make the necessary corrections and only infrequently making adjustments of her own. She had entered the descent plan into the system prior to initiating the sequence, and it was progressing normally.

Amelia studied the monitor. The screen displayed their position against a simple graphic of the ideal path. Beside the graphic was a column of constantly updating numbers. "Right on course," she said softly, almost to herself. "Altitude 20,000."

Claire took a moment to glance out the forward viewport. It was daylight. The sky was clear, tinged a dull tan color. The shuttle began to level out; the curve of the horizon crept up into view and the surface of the planet spread out below them; rolling dunes and downs and hollows brushed with dark brown swathes of shadow and rock. As they continued to descend, scrub brush and even a few scraggily trees became visible.

"Five miles to pod," stated Amelia.

Claire monitored their decreasing speed and continuing gradual descent. She prepared to take manual control of the shuttle. Seeing this, Amelia settled back into her seat, her harness self-adjusting.

"You sure?" she asked.

"Of course I'm sure."

Amelia gave a half-grin. "Not a problem."

"Good."

"Two miles," stated Amelia.

Claire flipped a switch, ran a fingertip across the keypad panel. "On manual."

Amelia had her eyes forward now, looking out at the terrain, which was quickly rising up to meet them.

"There's the pod," she said. The pod, an oblong capsule about fifty feet long, had settled into the sand at one end of a shallow hollow a thousand feet across. A rocky crag rose up behind it, forming a ridge that curved around to the left.

A cluster of short, rocky spires stood in the very center of the hollow.

Claire continued past the hollow, came around and guided the shuttle back in. She approached a wide, level spot opposite the central rock cluster from the pod. Hovering eighty feet above the surface, she pressed a keypad on the side panel. An indicator light came to life, turning amber. They both heard and felt the landing strut apparatus, unused for decades, open and shift and crank and begin to extend. The struts locked into position, the indicator light changed from amber to green.

Claire lowered the shuttle to the surface of Planet X.

Disengaging their safety harnesses, Amelia and Claire stood and looked out through the forward viewport. The shuttle was facing the center of the hollow. The rock formation stood about two hundred feet in front of them. They could see the pod another few hundred feet beyond, on the other side of the formation, and the rock wall rising up behind the pod. A sand-drift had pushed up against it, partially burying it.

The pod was just over fifty feet long, thirty feet in diameter, and had a smooth windowless surface.

"It's a standard supply pod," said Claire.

"Hmm." Amelia frowned. "It looks like you're going to get your walk."

After all this time in the shuttle, stepping out into the open was unnerving. No walls, no ceiling... the brownish gray shell of the sky overhead seemed way too far away. The ground beneath their feet was firmer than they expected. They discovered a hard surface beneath a thin layer of fine, gritty sand.

They were wearing light, one-piece suits designed for moderate conditions such as this. The suit would keep them from getting too hot or too cold. A simple face mask attached to a small oxygen canister would supplement the thin atmosphere.

Twelve steps from the shuttle, Claire whispered a satisfied *yes*, and skipped her next step. Glancing over at Amelia, her sister grumbled "yeah, yeah", the words muffled by the face mask over her mouth and nose.

They worked their way around the rock formation. It was clearly a natural formation, but it still managed to create the impression of some kind of primitive pagan monument. They continued forward, the pod now about a hundred feet directly ahead of them. From this distance it looked partially buried in the sand, which was surprising, now that they knew of the hard surface just beneath the thin layer of sand.

They approached the access hatch near one end of the pod. The bottom half of the door was buried in the drift of sand that had pushed up against the pod. Since the door opened outward, they would have to clear it away before they could get inside.

They dropped to their knees and began scooping with their gloved hands.

Amelia noted that considering the hard surface just below the sandy layer, the pod couldn't have half-buried itself in the sand during its landing. The sand that had collected against the side of the pod got there after the pod landed.

"Your point?" asked Claire. She was growing increasingly out of breath, digging deep into the sand and scooping it back with both hands.

"So it's a lot of sand," said Amelia. "It's like a major snow drift."

Claire was focused on clearing the door. "Uh, huh."

Amelia rose to her feet. She studied the scene around them. "Sand storm," she said. "On a serious scale."

"Uh, huh."

"This sand didn't come from here. It came from outside the basin."

"Whatever."

"It blows in from above, comes down into the hollow, and pushes up against the pod and the rock wall behind it."

"Whatever." Claire leaned back on her heels, looked sharply up at her sister. "A little help here."

One overhead light came on when they entered the pod. It did little to push the shadows from the main compartment. Still, it was enough light that they could see to get around, and that was the intent.

The room took up about half the width of the pod and a third the length. Along the wall beside them was the communications station. A small galley was set along the right wall. Next to the galley was the hatch leading aft to where the two main holds were located, as well as the enclosed engine compartment.

Amelia walked to the square table in the middle of the room. The systems console was inset into the surface. She activated the environmental systems. A few moments later the primary lighting came on, then the climate control systems.

"Okay, we're good," she said.

Claire waited a few moments, then pulled her face mask down and tested the air. She gave her sister a positive nod and then pulled her gloves off as she stepped through an opening in the wall directly opposite. It was a narrow room with bunks on the right, two doors on the left. One door led to the equipment room, the other to the toilet and shower compartment.

Coming back into the main compartment, she saw that Amelia had moved over to the communications station. Her sister glanced briefly in her direction as Claire continued toward the hatch leading to the aft compartments.

"I'll find Danny's message," said Amelia.

"I'll see what supplies he thought to send us," said Claire.

The aft section consisted of two holds set along the walls to either side, a sealed engine compartment in the center that ran to the end of the pod. Claire found a number of containers secured in the storage racks. A cursory inspection found rations, clothing, an assortment of spare parts for the shuttle, replacement equipment, and more than a few years worth of cryo-juice canisters.

Thank you, dear brother...

She would do a thorough inventory once they transferred the supplies to their shuttle. For now, Claire closed the last container and returned to the main compartment.

Amelia had brought a chair over to the communications station. There were only two chairs in the pod, and they were usually locked into position at one of the stations.

She spun slowly about when Claire came into the room, leaned back and looked up at her sister. She said nothing, but was wearing a curious expression. It was as though she wasn't quite sure what to say.

"Did you find his message?" asked Claire.

"Yeah," noncommittally.

"So?"

"It was easy enough to open. Same key."

"Amelia..."

Amelia gave Claire another uncertain look, finally spun slowly about again in her chair and reached out to the comm panel. She activated the recorded message without saying a word.

The screen flickered and Danny's face appeared on the monitor. He looked much older, decades older; and tired.

But what struck Claire most was the sadness in the eyes. That had never been there before.

"Hey, sisters one and two," he said. He tried to smile. "Hope you like the goodies I'm sending. Figure they'll come in handy."

"Absolutely," sighed Claire. "Thank you much."

"So... reason for the call. Don't go home. Not a good idea. There's no one there, or in any of the colonies. The bad guys have been busy. Their little war just goes on and on and, you know, they continue to conscript us and send us out to play soldier for them."

"But it's been decades," said Claire.

"So goes galactic-size wars," said Amelia.

Danny's message continued. He seemed to shift gears.

"Those of us remaining have retreated to Old Earth. An interesting place, actually. I don't know why we never visited before. Anyway... we've created what we call a Labyrinth Sphere. Think of it as a kind of defensive shield that encloses the Solar System."

Claire turned quickly to Amelia. "That had to have taken years."

"Like you said, Claire; the war has been going on for decades."

"There's one way in, one way out," Danny's message went on. "It takes a unique ID to enter, and the passage sequence through the labyrinth reconfigures behind each ship as it passes through. I'm sending an incomplete ID for you to enter into your shuttle's system. You'll need to modify it using our family code."

"Paranoid much?" mumbled Claire.

"This will give you your own unique valid ID. As you approach the labyrinth, the monitoring system will read this ID. Once it accepts it, it will send you the encoded current sequence that will get you through the labyrinth." Danny's expression grew deadly serious. "If the monitoring system doesn't accept the ID, or if you deviate from the path specified in the sequence, automatic weapons systems will destroy the shuttle without warning. So don't mess it up."

Danny leaned in nearer the screen. "Hope this message finds you, and I hope all is well. See you soon."

The screen went dark.

Claire hesitated, then looked over at the galley station. "All right, then. How about we get something to eat?"

"Meatloaf," suggested Amelia.

"Hard to tell. It might be." Claire had never been able to comprehend Amelia's fondness for that meat-flavored ration. She let it go, thought a moment then. "It'll be dark soon. No sense going back to the shuttle today. We should spend the night here."

The pod wasn't meant as living quarters, but it offered the basics and would serve in a pinch.

"I'm fine with that." Amelia stood and brought her hands together. "You cooking?"

The lighting throughout the pod was turned down low. There was a faint hum thrumming through the compartments, the sound of the environmental systems working to keep them warm and to cycle carbon dioxide for oxygen. Claire and Amelia were in the sleeping compartment, Claire in the upper bunk, Amelia the lower. They had been asleep for several hours, having gone to bed after a simple dinner and an evening of planning for the next day and some discussion of Danny's message.

They wouldn't be going to their home world, nor to their original destination at the time that everything had gone crazy. They would be going to Old Earth. Neither of them had ever been there. It had been an administrative world, holding the vast library of human knowledge, for centuries. Very few people had actually lived there.

Until now; now it held not only the wealth of human knowledge, but now it seemed much of free humanity as well.

How many? Danny hadn't said. Nor had he said how many the Takiree had conscripted or how many might still be alive.

If the rest of their family had passed on, Amelia and Claire hoped they had died free a long time ago. If they were yet alive, they had to have spent years in cryo, as had

Danny. If that was the case, they hoped they were on Old Earth.

But Danny had said nothing of the rest of the family.

Amelia rolled onto her back. After several moments, the relaxed expression on her face slowly morphed; the hint of something... intense thought, focus... concentration. Her eyes opened. She wasn't yet fully awake, but she was no longer asleep.

Something had roused her. Her head drifted slowly to one side. She looked about the sleeping compartment.

Nothing appeared out of the ordinary, and yet...

She looked out into the tiny room a few seconds more, finally pulled her blanket aside and brought her legs around, brought her feet to the floor and sat up. She listened for her sister in the upper bunk. Claire's breathing was normal; there was an occasional grumbling snore; also normal.

So what was wrong?

Amelia leaned forward and stood up. She took the single step into the middle of the small compartment. She looked about again, she listened.

There.

That sound. The background noise was different. There was a hissing noise; a faint hissing sound. It was pushing in on the sound of the environmental systems.

"Amelia?" Claire was awake in her bunk now, up on one elbow. She was looking at Amelia.

Amelia looked back to Claire, said nothing.

"What's that sound?" asked Claire.

"I don't know."

"Something wrong with environmental?"

"No. No, I don't think so." Amelia tilted her head, furrowed her brow. "It's coming from outside."

Claire sat up in the bunk, dropped to the floor. "That can't be good. We better check it out."

Amelia sat at one of the table's central consoles in the main compartment. She brought it to life, studied the monitor, worked again at the keyboard as Claire worked her way to the door.

"Six degrees," said Amelia. "Warmer than normal for around here, this time of night."

"Anything toxic?" Claire's hand rested on the latch. The hissing noise from outside continued to grow louder.

"All readings are showing clean."

That was good enough for Claire. She pushed down on the latch and pushed open the door; or tried to. The door was pushing back. A drift of sand blocked the bottom of the door. Claire laid her shoulder against it and managed to widen the opening enough get her body through.

A blinding wind was blowing and she quickly brought her arm up to protect her face. The air, bitterly cold, was filled with fine, gritty sand.

Six degrees Fahrenheit and near hurricane strength wind... the hissing sound was that of sand blowing against the shell of the pod.

Claire stepped back inside and closed the hatch.

"Are you all right?" asked Amelia. She was on her feet and had taken several steps toward her sister. Claire brushed cautiously at her face. Her skin looked as though she had rubbed coarse sandpaper across it.

"That hurt," she grumbled. Her hair, her clothes, and the entire forward section of the compartment, was covered in a layer of sand.

Amelia was looking closely at Claire. The grit had dug into her skin, leaving a hundred tiny red marks. "I'll get some warm water, and something to sterilize your uh... face."

Claire brushed at her clothes and hair. She managed to speak casually. "I think I figured out what that weird sound is."

"Ya think?" Amelia had gone to a cabinet and was looking through first aid supplies. "Interesting weather pattern; probably happens on a daily cycle across the planet; the sudden temperature change from day to night, maybe drifting high and low air pressure cells, maybe a combination of both."

"You have no idea, do you?"

"Not a clue." She set a small box on the counter, went over to the galley station to dampen a cloth. "But I'm pretty sure we won't be going outside after dark."

It was morning. All was quiet. Amelia stepped clumsily from the sleeping quarters into the main compartment. She had managed a few hours of restless sleep.

Claire was sitting at the central table hovering over a bowl. She looked briefly up at Amelia, returned to her breakfast. She spooned a mouthful of something gray before she spoke.

"The storm finally died down, about an hour ago," she said.

Amelia looked once to the galley station, then to the door. She decided... and started to the door. Claire waited until Amelia reached for the latch.

"We may have a little trouble getting out of here," she said. She took another spoonful of breakfast.

Amelia pushed at the door, managed only a few inches before stopping. She peaked through the narrow opening, then pulled the door closed.

Claire pointed at the door with her spoon. "Sand."

Amelia stared at the door. It was partially blocked by a sand drift. "So I see."

"Breakfast?" asked Claire. "The label says oatmeal. It isn't bad, really; if you're into oatmeal."

Claire just managed to squeeze her way through the partially opened door, still mostly blocked by the sand drift. Perhaps a lighter breakfast would have been wiser. She stepped away from the pod and stepped up beside Amelia.

The sky was clear and bright gray. There was the slight hint of a breeze.

Claire's attention shifted from the sky overhead down to their shuttle, sitting on the other side of the hollow, beyond the other side of the central rock formation. There were drifts of sand pushed up against the landing struts, but she wasn't able to see much else.

"Well, it looks to be in one piece," she said.

"The fewer nights here, the better."

"No argument there." Claire looked back over her shoulder. "What say we get the hatch open, get the supplies transferred over?"

"Now is when I'm thinking you should have parked a little closer."

Transferring the supplies from the pod to the shuttle was going to involve a number of trips. They didn't want to carry all those boxes and canisters by hand if they could help it. The only cart in the pod was the tool cart; the small wheels would bury in the sand, and it was too small to do much good anyway.

Using a thin metal shelf from one of the inventory racks, they came up with a makeshift sled to carry some of the larger boxes. This worked well enough once they figured the optimum weight load. Too heavy a load and the front end pushed into the sand, despite bending the nose at an angle.

So, larger but lighter boxes worked best. This meant that Claire could pull the sled on her own using a rope while Amelia followed alongside carrying several smaller boxes in her arms. This still meant they would be transferring inventory and supplies through much of the day.

Reaching the shuttle the first trip across, Claire left the sled near the hatch and conducted an initial inspection of the shuttle exterior while Amelia took the supplies inside. Working her way around the craft, she returned to the sled in time to meet her sister waiting to start back to the pod.

"Grit got into every strut joint," said Claire. "No permanent damage that I can see, but we'll have to get them cleaned out before we take off."

"Everything else look all right?"

"Two of the exposed satellite plates are scoured pretty bad. We should replace them."

"Which ones?" asked Amelia. Most of the external antennae and dishes had retracted prior to descending into the atmosphere, but several plates along the top-rear of the shuttle were fixed flat to the hull.

"Long range sensors." Claire gathered up the rope and prepared to pull the empty sled back to the pod. "And we should have closed the forward shield to protect the viewport."

"Oh, no... how bad?"

"Let's just say it's lost its crystal clear sheen." Claire started across the hollow toward the pod.

"It could have been worse, I guess," said Amelia, walking beside her. "I'll run di-ogs on all the systems soon as I get the chance."

"Engine compartment is fully protected, but they should get priority," said Claire. "If we can't get off the ground, nothing else matters."

Amelia figured that if <u>any</u> of the systems were down then nothing else mattered, but no sense nitpicking. "First on my list, then."

They returned to the pod and collected more of the supplies that Danny had sent them, loading the sled and collecting a couple of boxes that Amelia could carry.

Once they had finished their third run, Claire left Amelia to return to the pod on her own for more supplies while Claire set about cleaning the grit from the strut joints. They would need to be able to smoothly retract the landing gear once they lifted off.

Outside the pod, Amelia finished loading the sled and began tying down the boxes. Something caught her eye then, off to her left. She wasn't sure what it was, it had been little more than a shadow, but it was movement. She was sure of it.

She straightened and studied the landscape to her left... sand all the way to the perimeter of the hollow, where the rise sloped quickly up to a low crest. No sign of movement. No sign of anything. Listening, she heard only the faint whispering of the light breeze across the sandy floor of the hollow.

Finishing tying the boxes to the sled, Amelia pulled the rope taut, began drawing the sled along. Reaching the rock formation, she veered left and continued around the rocks.

She stopped.

She could have sworn she saw something out of the corner of her eye, a flickering shadow within or perhaps beyond the rock formation on her right.

Now though, as before, there was nothing.

Are my eyes playing tricks on me?

Maybe... or maybe there's something here with us.

The shuttle was directly ahead, about two hundred feet further on. Amelia leaned into the rope, again pulling it taut, and quickly made her way across to the ship, bringing the sled up beside the side hatch. Claire came around from the other side of the shuttle.

"The struts are clear," she said. "Just need to get those satellite plates replaced."

Amelia had dropped the rope and was looking back across the hollow to the rock formations. "Good," she said absently.

Claire had already started up the ramp into the shuttle to get the replacement plates. She stopped midway and looked back to her sister.

"Are you okay?"

"I guess," said Amelia.

"I don't think so. What's wrong?"

Amelia continued looking outward. "I think I saw something."

Claire looked outward now, took a step down the ramp. "Like what?"

"I don't know. Just... shadows, something moving..." she shrugged. "It's gone now."

Claire moved down beside her sister. "This place getting to you?"

"Maybe." Amelia shrugged again. "Probably."

Claire grew thoughtful. "How many more trips?"

"Three. Maybe four. Mostly cryo-juice canisters and the supplies in the cabinets."

"How 'bout I help you with that? Maybe shave off a trip. I can swap out the plates after."

"Sure," Amelia looked to Claire. "Let's do that."

§

The next two trips were uneventful. Amelia twice thought she saw something out of the corner of her eye, but each time she turned, the shadow quickly vanished and there was only the stillness. Claire had seen nothing and had begun to believe that this world was in fact getting to her little sister.

On this third and final trip, Claire came into the main compartment from the hold carrying a container. Amelia was emptying the cabinets, tossing the few odds and ends she found into a plastic bin.

"This is it from the hold," said Claire. She set the container on the table.

"And from here." Amelia carried the bin over and set it next Claire's container. "A few medical supplies, some galley stuff."

"A nice haul, wouldn't you say?" asked Claire. Looking around the room, the pod seemed strangely quiet. "Danny done good."

"He certainly knew just what we could use." Amelia sat at one of the chairs, then she too took a last look around the room. "It feels like we're forgetting something."

"We picked the place clean. You transferred the logs?"

"Danny's message was all there was. Still, I uploaded everything, in case he hid something in there somewhere."

"That would be Danny, all right."

The quiet of the pod pushed in on them. Amelia's expression grew solemn. At the time Danny had recorded the message, he had aged decades. He had spent a lot of time out of cryo.

And now... how old was their brother? And why had he said nothing of their uncle? Of their parents?

Amelia slid off the chair and stood before the systems control panel. It took a few moments to shut the environment down, then all systems. With that done, she picked up one of the containers and nodded in the direction of the hatch. Claire picked up the second container and led the way.

They made sure the hatch was closed and latched before starting across to the shuttle a final time. They had taken what supplies there were, but the pod itself could serve as an emergency shelter should anyone stumble across it and have need of it.

The world outside was as eerily quiet and still as the pod. As they worked their way toward the rock formation in the middle of the hollow, the late-afternoon sky began to grow steadily darker, a tint of brownish gray. As the moments passed and the darkness increased, it felt as though the sky overhead was pushing down on them. It was as a shell over the world.

"A storm's coming," said Claire.

"Not a good thing."

And then they began to hear something. It started as a dull, hissing sound, hardly above a whisper. And they could feel something brushing on their faces; a breeze. With it, the sound became a gritty, scratching noise.

"Look," said Amelia. She stopped. She was looking across the hollow to their right.

It was a little whirlwind, a spinning funnel of sand twelve feet high crawling slowly across the hollow like a tiny tornado.

"A dust devil," said Claire. "Is that what you saw before?"

"I don't know," said Amelia. "I mean, if it was, they vanished as soon as I turned to look at them."

Even as they watched, another one formed a few dozen yards from the first. Moments later, there was another.

It was getting busy in the hollow.

"C'mon." Claire started forward again, sounding a bit anxious. She had no idea what these dust devils might portend, and she didn't really care to find out.

They made their way around the rock formation, picked up the pace as they hurried across to the shuttle. Claire opened the hatch and went inside. Amelia stopped at the opening and turned to look back the way they had come.

There were dust devils creeping about all over the hollow, twisting and writhing, sand drawn up and forming the slithering funnels. One dust devil would wither away just as two others formed.

The gray sky overhead continued to grow darker.

Claire returned to the airlock with a pair of satellite panels just as Amelia closed the outer hatch.

"You need to open that back up, Sis," she said. "I gotta get these plates installed."

"We should leave now," said Amelia.

"Give me five minutes. Ten tops," said Claire. "I'd rather not do this EVA."

Amelia stared coolly at her sister. She knew that replacing those plates would take at least twenty, probably longer. Still... doing it now would be easier, and EVAs had inherent risks.

She opened the hatch and returned to the main compartment.

Claire had to open a narrow panel to expose foot holds in order to get atop the craft and work her way aft. Both of the damaged plates were near the rear of the shuttle. She wore her face mask, but could feel the bite of blowing sand on her exposed cheeks. Dropping to one knee, she quickly removed the first damaged plate using the tool attached to her utility belt.

Only after completing the first installation did she stand and take a look around her. From atop the shuttle, it looked as though the dozen or more dust devils were dancing around the rock formation in the center of the hollow, weaving their way in and around the massive stones. Across the way, the pod was now barely visible.

Claire worked her way quickly over to the second satellite plate. This one took a little longer. The wind was continuing to pick up, the blowing sand made the detail work more difficult.

Back to ground on the sand, she closed the footholds panel and worked her way back to the hatch. One last look out across the hollow... the dust devils seemed almost alive.

Returning inside, she found Amelia sitting at the computer station in the main compartment. She was listening to Danny's message, probably for the fifth time.

"Gleaning anything new?" she asked.

Amelia reached over and turned off the message. She leaned back and stared at the now blank monitor.

"How old d'you figure he was there, Claire? Fifty? Older?"

"Fifty is about right," said Claire softly. "He's spent some time in cryo."

"Some." Amelia spoke without turning from the monitor. "And since then? Since he recorded that?"

"I hope so. I like to think so."

Amelia nodded slowly. Everyone they had known was probably long dead. She desperately hoped Danny had gone into cryo after posting the message and sending the pod on its way.

"I guess we ought to get out of here." She hadn't yet brought herself back to the here-and-now, but knew that she needed to.

"Yep." Claire waited for her sister to stand, to make a move toward the cockpit.

"Yeah," sighed Amelia. It took her another few moments to come completely out of her reverie. More determined then, she slid back in her chair and stood up. "Yes. Yes. Get your butt into the driver's seat and get us off this planet."

Once in the cockpit, Claire buckled herself into the pilot's chair, Amelia the co-pilot. Claire had already entered the take-off sequence into the nav system, so it was simply a matter of bringing it online.

Amelia brought the internal systems up. "Good to go when you are," she said.

Claire said nothing, continued swiping displays and pressing keypads.

Amelia leaned back, kept an eye on the monitors while looking out the forward viewport. The air in the hollow was growing heavy with grit; the wind was growing stronger and increasingly erratic. A dust devil appeared to walk past the front of the shuttle.

She tried to ignore the quickly building storm. "Old Earth," she said calmly. "I always wanted to go there. Always planned on it, one day."

"You would," said Claire. "Old books and dusty history."

Amelia smiled thinly. "Much more than that, Claire. Forests and oceans, mountains and rivers and snow and sun."

They both knew that Old Earth's environment had mostly recovered from a manmade climate disaster. They had pulled back from the brink soon enough that over time they had been able to bring the planet back.

The planet of humanity's birth, buried now deep within this Labyrinth Sphere that Danny had described.

"Okay, Sis... next stop, palm trees and quiet lagoons," said Claire. She completed processing the liftoff sequence, swiped the panel and initiated the procedure.

Amelia felt herself pushed into her seat as the shuttle lifted from the surface. The scene outside, rock formation and shallow hollow, fell quickly away, and the world suddenly spread out for miles in all directions. The gray sky overhead crept down to the distant horizon in a great curving shell. Massive, rolling clouds of brown were sweeping across the landscape in enormous sandstorms.

Claire felt the landing struts retracting. She watched the indicator light, waiting for it to signal the gear successfully locking and the doors closing.

"Landing struts retracted," she stated then, and continued to monitor their ascent trajectory. "On path, on course."

Amelia noted that the highest of the storms was now below them. The horizon was far off and falling away as they continued to climb upward. Above them, the gray was quickly growing to dark. As the backdrop grew increasingly black, stars began to appear.

Just as Amelia began to feel weightless and her safety harness pulling at her, the shuttle's gravity plating engaged. A few moments later, Claire calmly stated that they were in orbit. She was already initiating the sequence to take them out of orbit.

"Twelve minutes to departure," she said. Claire had entered the navigation calculations to take them from Planet X to a safe position outside the Sol system light years distant. This had been timed to the orbit departure sequence and would initiate immediately after they left orbit.

"Twelve minutes," repeated Amelia. She began checking all internal systems, verifying they were good to go. If anything was seriously wrong, better to stay in orbit and resolve it here, or, if absolutely necessary, return to the planet's surface.

The interior of the cabin suddenly grew bright, it took several seconds for the viewport glass to auto-dim.

The shuttle's orbit had brought them around the planet, its sun born now on the horizon, the bright rays were streaking across the globe, the star aglow against the black of space.

Claire finished her preparations, sat back and took in the scene. It was soothing, serene. It always affected her this way.

Amelia finished her di-ogs half a minute later.

"All green," she said. She glanced over at Claire when there was no reply. She looked then out the forward viewport. Despite the slight scouring the glass had taken on the planet, it was indeed a beautiful sight. "We're good to go."

Claire managed a quick check of her panels.

"Two minutes," she said, rested her head against the seatback.

"Ready in two," said Amelia distractedly.

One last sunrise before the long journey to Old Earth.

Episode Six

"Labyrinth"

Occasional faint beeps and tweets were the only sounds that broke the blanket silence in the shuttle's cockpit. There was no sound of human activity, there was no muffled rumble of engines; nothing but the quiet existence of the shuttle's computer system going about its solitary business.

The only illumination came from tiny indicator lights on the front panel set below the forward viewport and those in the console between the two empty seats; that and what little light managed to reach into the cockpit through the narrow opening leading down to the main cabin.

The main compartment was lit only by the soft glow of the panels set beneath the pair of sleeper canisters that were recessed into the port wall, set behind clear plastic panels. Claire lay in the upper canister, her sister Amelia in the lower. They were dressed in their beige coveralls, the monitoring and bio tubes attached to the synthetic sleeves and at the waist. They lay comfortably asleep on thick cryo-support sleeper pads.

In the cockpit, several alert lights flashed. A series of soft beeping sounds broke the silence and a small, square panel that had lain dormant for years began to glow. Back in the main cabin, the overhead lighting turned on, set to low and providing minimal illumination. The panel below the sleeper canisters came to life and changes were made to the fluids that fed the occupants through the bio tubes. Adjustments to cabin life support were made in preparation of the passengers' awakening.

§

Each canister's clear wall panel slid aside. A few moments later, Claire and Amelia opened their eyes. They lay unmoving, blinking, staring uncertainly above them. Amelia finally rolled onto her side and sat up, brought her bare feet down onto the floor. She took in several long breaths as she looked about the main compartment, absently detached the support tubes from her coveralls. She looked side-glance at a pair of feet that appeared suddenly beside her, attached to legs dangling from the upper bed.

"Why do those feet have to be the first thing I see every time I come out of cryo?" asked Amelia.

"One of life's little quirks, little sister." Claire looked about the cabin, then up at the alert light. It wasn't flashing. Good sign; so this was likely the scheduled awakening, then. This was their third since leaving Planet X. Only once had they been awakened due to an issue the ship couldn't resolve on its own.

Claire slid down from the upper cryo-bed, steadied herself as she leaned on the panel. "I feel older," she growled. She looked down at her sister. "Do I look older?"

"You are so not a morning person," said Amelia, a jibe usually directed to her. She leaned forward and stood up. Giving herself a moment to gain her balance, she shuffled over to the water dispenser. "One of us should see where we are."

If this was in fact the scheduled wake-up call, they should be several weeks outside the Solar System, still well outside the Labyrinth Sphere that was protecting Old Earth.

"Yeah, you go do that," said Claire, not yet ready to push off from the cryo-beds.

"I'm thirsty," said Amelia, filling a cup with water. "And I gotta pee."

That was of course totally not true. The cryo-system took care of all that, so there was no way she needed to take care of business immediately coming out of cryo. Yet this was always Amelia's first item of business upon waking. Claire had long ago given up arguing with her about it. It wasn't worth it. Amelia had it in her head and it didn't really matter.

"Fine. I'll see you up front," said Claire. She headed for the cockpit as Amelia went aft.

The view beyond the cockpit was a splash of stars, Old Earth's sun being just one more at this distance. There was nothing out there to indicate the Labyrinth Sphere.

Claire first brought up the nav systems. The monitor came alive, detailing current location, course and other data. Nothing scary there; she brought up sensors next.

Amelia came in and sat in the seat opposite as Claire began reviewing the data. "So?" she asked.

"Right on course," said Claire. "Exactly where we're supposed to be; give or take."

"Give or take?" Amelia smiled. She began activating internal sensors.

"A light year here or there."

"Right..." A light year here or there could have been dangerous.

"Twelve days from the coordinates Danny gave us."

"So, right where we're supposed to be," said Amelia.

"I think I just said that."

They had planned to come out of cryo twelve days from Danny's coordinates, giving themselves a significant buffer when approaching the labyrinth. They certainly didn't want to hit the labyrinth while still in cryo.

Amelia leaned back and looked up from her monitors. If she didn't know to look for it, she would have been hard-pressed to point out which of those stars was Old Earth's sun.

She brought her attention back to the monitors. This latest period in cryo had lasted fourteen and a half years. The few systems issues that had arisen during that time had been easily resolved by the shuttle's primary system.

This was a good ship.

"Internal systems all look good."

"External systems good; navigation good," said Claire. "We're good."

"I like it," said Amelia.

Claire swung around in her seat. "Let's go have lunch."

§

They had been out of cryo for three and a half days, and all had been quiet. Amelia set her cup on the counter and settled again at the computer station in the main cabin. She spent most of her time in the main cabin.

"Oh boy," she mumbled. She moved back from the station and looked forward. "Oh, sister..."

"Yeah?" came faintly from the cockpit.

"Message coming in." Amelia stood and headed for the cockpit. Dropping into the copilot's seat, she transferred the communications station forward and brought it up. "Both audio and text."

"Let's hear it," said Claire.

Amelia tapped at the keypad. An unfamiliar voice came through the speaker, the words dry and emotionless.

"You have been targeted. If you do not have prior authorization, do not approach. Turn back now. This is the only warning you will receive. If you do not have prior authorization, you will be destroyed. There will be no further communication."

Amelia pressed the key a second time. "That's all there be. A recorded message, triggered by our approach."

"All right," Claire sighed and folded her arms. "Now what?"

"I figure next we'll get the request for the authorization code."

Danny had sent them part of the code that would gain them passage into the labyrinth. In the event someone other than Claire and Amelia had stumbled across his message, the code had been incomplete. Danny had told them the rest of it was part of a cryptography game they had played when they were younger. Amelia had sorted it out and completed the code after leaving Planet X, before they went into cryo.

Claire rested her head against the back of her seat. She looked over at her sister.

"So we wait," she said. She closed her eyes.

She may have fallen asleep, she wasn't sure. It may have been several minutes, was more likely several hours. Her sister's calm voice brought her awake.

"Something's coming in," said Amelia.

Claire slid around and stood up, moved over to stand behind Amelia. She leaned in and looked at the monitor. Lines of text were quickly scrolling up the screen, so quickly that it was impossible to catch more than a word or series of numbers here and there.

"What's it doing?" she asked.

"Request," said Amelia. "Asking for something."

Claire watched the monitor flicker and a block of data suddenly splash on the screen.

"How does our system know what to—"

"There was a handshake and the labyrinth got permission to look into one of our file systems."

"How can it do that? It shouldn't be able to do that."

"I don't know," said Amelia. "But I'm guessing it's probably a good thing."

The screen went quiet. After several uncomfortable seconds, another line of text displayed.

"Process complete," said Amelia.

The monitor went dark then. Claire moved back to her seat and sat down.

"Well?" she asked.

"If we don't die, I expect next we'll get the route."

There was half a minute of heavy silence, and it felt even longer. One of Amelia's monitors came alive then. She straightened and leaned forward.

"Here it comes," she said and began swiping at the keypads. She studied the screen.

Claire stretched to look at Amelia's screen.

"This is it, all right." Amelia began keying. "I'm sending it to you."

Claire shifted forward and brought up helm. She worked the keypanel, and after several seconds brought up navigation.

"Our entry point into the labyrinth sphere is a full two days away at current speed," she said, and continued processing their course into nav. Once entered, she keyed in the final sequence and was about to turn away when something caught her attention. She brought up the leftmost monitor and studied the data displayed.

"What is it?" asked Amelia.

"I'm not sure, but I think we're being followed."

"Good guys or bad guys?"

"I'm not getting any details, but whatever it is, it's closing on us."

"They gotta be bad guys."

Claire studied the helm data, finally nodded imperceptibly. "Good guys, bad guys or big, scary rocks, we should enter the labyrinth well ahead of them."

Amelia woke from a sound sleep, rolled slowly over in her bunk and sat up. She pushed her hair back and looked over at Claire. Her sister was sitting at the table, looked to be eating her breakfast.

"Good morning, little sister," said Claire. She took another bite of breakfast.

"Good morning," said Amelia. "What has you up so early? You're never up before me."

"Today's the day."

Amelia stood and started toward the water dispenser. "You're not worried, are you? It should be a breeze."

"Not a bit. Looking forward to it. A breeze."

Amelia filled a cup and leaned back against the counter. "Anything new on whatever's following us?"

"Getting closer. Still no communications; nothing. I'm not sure it's manned."

"Some sort of probe?"

"Probe, ship, weapon." Claire shrugged. "It's not any configuration I can identify."

"Bad guy, then."

"Who's to say? We've been gone a long time. Technology marches on. It might be one of ours, and just happens to be on the same course as us."

"But you don't think so."

"Not really." Claire pushed her plate aside and stood up. "Whatever or whoever it is, we'll be well into the labyrinth before it reaches us." She swallowed the last of her juice and took her breakfast dishes to the cleaning station. Amelia set her water cup onto the counter beside her sister.

"I gotta get cleaned up." she started aft.

"Make it quick, Amelia. You don't want to miss the big finish."

Once in the cockpit, Claire began making preparations to enter the labyrinth, including calculating speed and trajectory. This would take them through the first leg of the traverse. They were to be provided the course and speed of each leg of the route as they reached the end of each segment.

This meant that Claire would be navigating them through the labyrinth manually.

And that was totally okay with her.

She heard Amelia come into the cockpit and settle into the other seat. Neither said anything as Claire continued the prep work. Amelia brought her own systems up, transferring them from the computer station in the main cabin up to the cockpit. She then leaned back in her seat and waited for Claire to finish.

It took Claire another few minutes, then she too relaxed. She said nothing, laid her head back and gazed outward.

Amelia started to say something, decided it didn't matter. The sisters spent the morning quietly contemplating what was to come.

It was sometime before lunch when Claire finally sat forward and focused all her attention on the helm.

"We're in the labyrinth," she stated calmly.

Amelia was looking out the forward viewport. Not much there. Everything looked the same.

"Really?" she smirked. "And how can you tell?"

"Funny." Claire was focused on monitoring the helm.

"Sure," sighed Amelia. "I can do that, sometimes..."

They were nearing the end of the first leg of this first segment of the labyrinth. Claire acknowledged Amelia, took the mug her sister offered and set it into the holder without taking a drink.

She was getting ready for the course change. The labyrinth monitoring system that was watching them was fully automated. Removing the human element took out all the guess work, but it also took out the... human element. A human might be able to take into account an innocent misstep. The automated monitoring system watching their every move would not.

Amelia meanwhile had taken to tracking the ship that was following them. It would be entering the labyrinth within minutes, and was following their trajectory exactly.

"Oh, well isn't that interesting?" she asked.

"I wouldn't know," said Claire absently. "Not without a little more info."

"There's a second ship following the ship that's following us."

Claire had to let that interesting little tidbit go for the moment. She had things to do.

"Initiating course change," she said. She worked quickly at the keypad, then closely monitored their trajectory. It was a full minute before she visibly relaxed. She took a drink from her mug.

"Is the second ship *with* the first or *going after* the first?" she asked.

"I suppose we'll know in a minute," said Amelia. She continued to work with and closely monitor the data coming in through the ship's sensors.

That minute passed, and then another.

"Whoa," she said suddenly. Their sensors had identified an energy burst coming from what must have been a monitoring platform that was invisible to all sensors. Almost immediately afterward, the first ship following the shuttle disintegrated. It had been there in the sensors, and then it was gone.

Amelia started to explain to Claire what she had seen, then stopped just as suddenly.

Sensors identified weapons' fire emitted from the second ship, targeting the monitoring platform. The process repeated itself when a second invisible platform immediately took out the second ship.

The shuttle's sensors quieted then, continuing to monitor the once again peaceful labyrinth.

"Talk to me, Amelia," said Claire. Something had apparently happened, but her sister hadn't said anything beyond *whoa.*

"Well..." Amelia said hesitantly. "We don't have to worry about being followed. And... our route through the labyrinth does indeed appear to be closing behind us."

She described the first ship being destroyed, then the second ship destroying the monitoring platform, only to then also be destroyed by a second platform.

Claire thought about that a few moments, then let out a quiet *hmmph.*

"What *hmmph?*" asked Amelia.

"I don't think those ships were trying to get through the labyrinth at all," said Claire. "I think they were probes looking to take out the weapons platforms, to weaken the labyrinth."

"Hmmph," said Amelia. So the probes followed them into the labyrinth, the first probe serving as bait to track the location of one of the invisible platforms, and the second takes it out. "I would say testing defenses, the viability of bait and shoot. If it was just to weaken the labyrinth, they'd be coming in with a whole line of probes."

"That may be happening soon enough. I hope there are human eyes monitoring all this from somewhere, seeing what they're up to."

"Meanwhile, back on the farm," mumbled Amelia. "Does this change our situation in the slightest?"

"Other than not being followed by bad guys?" asked Claire. "Not a particle."

Amelia sat alone in the cockpit, relaxed, half-turned in her seat with one foot on the lower step of the central console. She could hear her sister down in the main cabin making her lunch.

She was hardly paying attention to the data coming in on the external sensors. The shuttle had passed a number of outposts en route through the labyrinth, all of them abandoned. Some had been located on moons of the planets they passed, others were stations orbiting the moons.

They were now within the inner planets of the Solar System, having crossed the Mars orbit several weeks earlier. Amelia expected to start seeing sensor data of Old Earth in the next ten hours. It would be sketchy at first, but would grow more detailed as they drew nearer the birth world of humanity.

Claire came back into the cockpit, her lunch in hand. She gave a casual glance to her own monitors as she sat down and began eating.

They usually ate at the table in the main cabin, even during these weeks in the labyrinth, but they were traveling a section where they thought it best to maintain a vigil in the cockpit and be ready for anything. During such times, it just felt more comfortable being there.

Claire glanced again at data coming in.

"I was right," she said, and took another bite of her lunch.

"The space station?" asked Amelia.

"Yep."

The route they had been given for the final leg of the route through the labyrinth didn't take them directly to Old Earth. It instead would take them to a large space station several hundred thousand miles from Earth, just inside the orbit of the Earth's moon.

"You think it's another security layer?" asked Amelia. She still had one foot on the central console, her head resting against the back of her seat. She was staring out at the dark.

"Maybe," said Claire. "I just know it's where we're headed."

She continued eating her lunch, gave a nod to Amelia to go get something to eat. Her sister sat up with a loud sigh, stood and headed back into the main cabin.

Unlike her sister, Amelia felt no strong compulsion to return to the cockpit. They spent way too much time forward so far as she was concerned, and she was perfectly content to let Claire keep an eye on things for a while. She settled in at the table to eat.

Barely ten minutes later, Claire was calling her forward. Claire wouldn't do that unless it was important.

Amelia returned to the cockpit and slid back into her seat. She noted an indicator light on one of her panels and a flashing row of text on a monitor. "An incoming message," she said.

Claire looked at her sister without turning her head. "You think maybe that's why I asked you to come on back?"

Amelia ignored the sarcasm and began pressing keys on the key panel.

"It's coming from the station," she said.

"Hmm... then maybe you should answer it."

"Text only. What is it with these people?" Amelia continued working the keyboard panel. Half a minute later her left monitor scrolled with rows of data and text.

"What's the word?" asked Claire.

A few more seconds, then, "They bid us welcome," said Amelia. "After that, it's all about new trajectory and velocity, and a directive to then prepare to disengage helm and accept tracking system."

"They're bringing us in?"

"I'm sending the data over to you," said Amelia. "Once we're on trajectory with designated course and speed, they'll take over."

Claire studied the data as she began entering calculations into navigation. According to the data, they would hand control over to the station in seven hours, when they would be arriving at the specified coordinates. She had no way of knowing how long it would then take to track them in. They might bring them in at a dead crawl.

She finished entering their new course into the nav system. "Here we go," she said and swiped a fingertip across the keypad.

Amelia was feeling uncomfortable, but didn't really know why. After all, in a few weeks, maybe as little as a few days, this decades-long journey would be over. She and Claire would no longer be alone.

Would Danny be there? Was anyone in their family still alive?

Amelia closed her eyes and laid her back. She gave a quiet sigh.

Please be there. Danny, be there...

Claire and Amelia stood in their shuttle's airlock, waiting for the hatch sensors to verify the environment on the other side. They had still had no communication with a live person. The automated docking had gone smoothly enough, but for all they knew, the space station had a population of zero and was open to space. The sisters were dressed in their work coveralls. They would rather not get into EVA suits, but that depended on the readings that came back.

A small panel next to the hatch flickered to life and data splashed on the screen.

Everything came back good. Even the temperature was comfortable.

"That's a good sign, anyway," said Claire. She opened the hatch and they stepped into the umbilical tube connecting the shuttle to the station. There was no one waiting for them in the station's airlock. Claire reached out to her left and pressed the hand panel that closed the hatch behind them.

The clicking sound of the hatch locking drifted into the heavy quiet of the station.

"Well, this is unsettling," said Amelia. "And eerily familiar."

"Hopefully no ghosts this time," said Claire. The ship they had come across so many years ago hadn't actually had ghosts, but close enough...

"I just want people," said Amelia. "I want to talk to somebody and have him talk back."

"Beware what you wish for, little sister."

"I'll take my chances," said Amelia.

The two of them moved deeper into the station. The only sounds they heard were those of the environmental systems working to keep the station habitable. Overhead, lighting bands recessed in the passageway ceiling were set to medium soft and provided just enough light to push back the shadows.

This part of the station held gear closets, equipment closets, changing rooms, and showers. There was no one in any of them, but unless there was an EVA planned or recently completed, that was to be expected.

They turned down the next passage. It was as dead quiet as the last.

"Hello?" called Claire. That single word was jarring in the silence.

They continued walking, looking into every room they passed. The station was big.

"Claire, I'm really getting a bad feeling about this," said Amelia.

"Oh, I passed *bad feeling* way back, sister," said Claire.

They stepped into a medium-sized mess hall. There were a dozen tables scattered about the room, a long food counter ran along the back wall, and there were water and drink dispensers to the right.

"There's no one here, Claire," said Amelia. She worked her way over to the food counter, stepped around behind it. "We have boxes and seal-packs back here. This place is well stocked."

Claire moved over to a comm station mounted on the wall to their left. She picked up the receiver, keyed in a number that she read from the list hanging beside the cradle. After a few seconds, she tried another; and then another.

No response.

She finally pushed the open mic. "I'm calling anyone in the station. Please respond." They could hear her voice broadcasting throughout the station. "Anyone in the station. We have two ladies recently arrived from the outer reaches, looking for a little friendly conversation. Anybody here?"

She waited a full ten seconds, looked over at Amelia and set the receiver back in the cradle.

"All right," she said, one hand still resting on the receiver. "Let's find the command center."

The command center was larger than their entire shuttle. There were half a dozen operations console stations, the commander's station, even a rudimentary helm that allowed the crew to maneuver the station when necessary.

And there was no one there.

Amelia went looking for communications as Claire went to the commander's station. She sat in the commander's chair and swung a console around, began typing at the keypad and watched the small monitor. After a minute or more, she pushed the console aside.

"Nothing in the commander's log," she said. "I mean nothing. Empty. Nada." She slid out of the chair and moved over to a bank of operations stations. She tried one and then another until she found the science station.

Amelia continued to work at the comm station. "I'm not finding much in communications," she said, hovering over the panel. "I do see the station's communications activity with us, and the automated messaging."

"That's it?"

"Just a minute." Amelia frowned as she studied the info she was digging through. "There is one interesting thing... I see the exact same set of transmissions three times previous to ours."

"So we're not the first, then."

"No, we're not. However," Amelia looked up from the panel, looked over at her sister. "In the last thirty five years, there have been only those three others. There's not a lot of traffic coming through here."

According to both the station chronometer and their own internal body clocks, it was getting late. Claire and Amelia had a quick meal and then sought out a room in the station's sleeping quarters to spend the night. Despite expectations, both managed to get a good night's sleep. The small room was clean, the beds comfortable. They found clean sheets and blankets in a nearby supply closet.

When Claire woke the next morning, she found Amelia already up and gone. She cleaned up and dressed, then walked the empty passageways to the mess hall. She found a breakfast ration packet and heated it, ate a quiet breakfast on her own before heading up to the command center.

Amelia was sitting at the science station when Claire reached command. Claire went directly to the commander's station and dropped into the chair.

"What'd you find, Amelia?" Claire turned slowly about. "Are we supposed to just wait? Should we head down to the planet on our own? What happens if we try? I wouldn't want to get shot out of the sky as we entered the atmosphere."

Amelia looked both confused and unhappy. "Sensor readings have been giving back some odd data, and I'm not sure what to make of it."

"Which sensors?"

"I've been taking a look at Old Earth." Amelia frowned, curled her brow as she continued to study the sensor data. "The planet looks... deserted."

"Is it habitable?"

"Absolutely. Flora, fauna, oxygen, oceans... there's just no one there."

"Could they be hiding?"

"Theoretically possible, I suppose; somehow masking their presence." Amelia thought on that for a moment, then shook her head. "I don't think there's anybody home, Claire."

Claire nodded, spun slowly about in the command chair, her fingers drumming on the armrest. She mumbled loudly. "So what's the labyrinth for? What's this station for?"

And what about the three ships that came here before us? wondered Amelia. *Where did they go?*

She watched Claire absently tapping the armrest of the command chair. "So, waddya think, Claire?"

"I think..." Claire said softly, "that we were directed here for a reason. We don't appear to be in any immediate danger, so until we know more, we hang out here."

"Not that we have many options," said Amelia. "We can't go back the way we came."

Maneuvering the labyrinth was definitely out. Old Earth appeared open to them, but that wasn't a certainty. Something bad could be laying in wait. Even attempting to leave the station could trigger another of the hidden weapon platforms.

"That is correct," said Claire. "The way we came is probably not an option."

"And so we hang out here," sighed Amelia.

"For a bit."

Amelia passed through the umbilical tube and stepped into their shuttle. She worked her way forward and entered the main cabin. Rummaging through the galley station, she found a ration packet of meatloaf.

Two days without meatloaf was two days too long.

She turned about and was ready to head back into the station when she stopped, looked back behind her at the main computer station.

An indicator light was blinking.

She sat at the computer and activated the monitor. A pass code box displayed in the middle of the screen, waited patiently.

Amelia stared at the box, frowned thoughtfully. She twitched her mouth from one cheek to the other. Deciding then, she leaned forward and entered their now familiar family code. She hesitated, then clicked transmit.

Danny's face appeared on the screen.

"If you're seeing this, it means you've docked at Station Delta. Glad you made it." Danny should have looked more pleased. "Hello, by the way."

Hurrying down the passageways, Amelia found Claire in the space station's recreation room. Both of them had been spending quite a bit of time working with the exercise equipment over the previous days.

That, and just hanging out.

"There you are," said Claire. "Where ya' been?"

"Shuttle," said Amelia, waving her ration packet.

"Meatloaf? Geez, Amelia."

"Yeah. And um... a message from Danny."

"I'm assuming it has nothing to do with the meatloaf."

Amelia moved over and sat on a workout bench opposite her sister. She stared down at her hands for a long moment, finally looked up at Claire.

"It looks like we still have a ways to go."

Danny had recorded the message more than forty years earlier. At the time of the recording, the labyrinth had been fully functional for only a handful of years, and Old Earth had a refugee population of several hundred thousand.

But things were about to change. Danny wasn't quite sure how it was all going to turn out.

Human populations had grown scarce in this corner of the galaxy. The Takiree had recently stumbled across the Solar System and Old Earth, and discovered the Labyrinth. They spent several years looking for weaknesses. According to Danny, they became obsessed with it, in their own alien way. They buzzed about the outer perimeter, poking and prodding. There was something in their DNA, in the way their brains were wired. The very idea of a labyrinth and the reward of Old Earth at its heart drove them crazy.

Most recently, they had begun sending probes into the Labyrinth.

And then things grew quiet.

Danny thought it may have been due to something happening back in their own corner of the galaxy. He couldn't imagine anything else drawing their focus away from their obsession with getting through the Labyrinth and reaching Old Earth.

That was when the Council came up with a new plan.

"Plan?" asked Claire.

"Plan..." sighed Amelia. She hesitated. She took in a long breath and let it out slow. "They left."

"Left? They left?"

"I'm afraid so."

"How could they leave? I mean, how could they just... leave?"

"Danny was a bit sketchy on that," said Amelia.

The population that had settled on Old Earth was certain the bad guys would return, given their earlier determination. And sooner or later they would find a way through the Labyrinth.

So, let them. It might take them years to get through to Old Earth, only to find it empty.

And while the Takiree fought and sacrificed and died getting through the Labyrinth, the refugees will have settled somewhere else.

Some of them, that is.

It took a considerable amount of time and resources for the population to secretly withdraw, but they did it. Some of them had gone to another out-of-the-way planet.

Many, however, had chosen a different path.

They were following after a huge human armada that was heading for the war in the far corner of the galaxy. But they weren't going to join the fight. They had gone to free their brethren, those who had been collected by the Takiree and forced to fight their war for them.

"This all happened a long time ago," said Claire. She hesitated a moment then. "Whatever was going to happen, already did."

"Probably. You were thinking of going after them?"

"Not really. I expect they're on their way back. If they... you know." Claire stared down at her hands. "I suppose Danny had thoughts on what we should do."

"He was a bit vague, really. He didn't know how long it would take for us to get here. He was leaning towards us following the refugees that were settling on that out of the way planet he mentioned, but he didn't know what the bad guy situation would be like when we got here."

Claire straightened her back, took a breath. "Can't have us leading the Takiree to the new home."

"That was the gist of it. So, what are we going to do?"

Claire looked about the exercise room. "Well, as for me, I think I'll finish my workout. Then lunch."

Amelia left Claire to her exercises, took her meatloaf ration packet to the mess hall and heated it. After lunch she returned to the command center and spent the afternoon going through science logs, comm logs and anything else she could find that might help her gain a better understanding of what had happened forty years earlier.

There wasn't much. Even the exact location of the planet the humans had chosen to migrate to was cryptic. It would take Amelia time to decipher, should that be where she and Claire decided to go.

Of the three previous visits to the station, it appeared one had been Danny. The other two, from all indications, had attempted to leave back through the Labyrinth, most likely following after the refugees.

When her stomach began its daily late afternoon grumbling, Amelia went in search of Claire. They had tended toward more traditional sit-down evening meals together since coming aboard the station, and she wanted to know what Claire wanted to do about dinner.

Her sister wasn't in any of her normal haunts, and Amelia was about to call for her over the intercom when she found herself in a narrow side-passage she hadn't gone into before. This led her to a long, narrow observation room; its outer wall was set with a series of tall, clear panels looking out into space.

Old Earth hung large against the black.

Claire was sitting on one of several benches, her back to the door.

Amelia came up behind her. "Wow."

Claire didn't respond. Amelia stepped around and sat on the bench beside her sister. They sat quiet for a long while, looking out beyond the station, out at the planet barely two hundred thousand miles away, a blue and white globe set against the jet-black of space.

"What do we do, Claire?" Amelia asked at last.

Claire didn't answer at first, and Amelia thought she wasn't going to answer at all. She finally did let out a gentle breath and spoke softly.

"What are our options, really?"

They sat silent again, taking in the view of Old Earth, bright and radiant... alive.

There was no hurry.

They had all the time in the universe.

Episode Seven

"Arrival"

The lighting in Cryo Room 3 was set to medium, creating a soft glow that was just bright enough to push away the shadows. Several of the transport ship's personnel were helping recently awakened sleepers from their cryo chambers. Colonel Dan Bradford, sitting on the edge of his cryo bed, waved away an approaching assistant, giving a polite thank you.

He rubbed at his face as he looked about. Of the twelve beds in this room, four were open, including his. The other eight remained in cryo state. That would indicate that this was probably his scheduled wake up call. The staff assisting the others from cryo were certainly calm enough.

Danny finished disconnecting his cryo-feed and monitor lines and stood up. His first few steps were slow and easy. By the time he reached the open doorway and stepped into the hall, he was steady enough to walk without the support of the nearby walls. Walking the hallway, he passed the open doorways of the other cryo rooms before stepping into the locker room. He found his locker, undressed and went into the showers.

His battalion had spent twenty two months in the war zone. His and the other human battalions had joined forces with the Jaung in their fight against the Takiree. It hadn't always gone well, but after almost two years they had accomplished their goal of freeing the hundreds of thousands of humans that had been taken over the span of two centuries and involuntarily conscripted to fight for the Takiree.

It had been messy. And even then it hadn't really been over. The Takiree chased them for two more years as they worked their way out of the quadrant. Eventually though, with the help of the Jaung, the humans were finally, truly on their way home.

Danny never did discover the reason for the war between Takiree and Jaung, but the Takiree were definitely on his own personal bad guys list. To be honest though, the Jaung were as scary to Danny as were the Takiree.

Cleaned up and dressed, he worked his way to the central passageway and started forward to the command deck. The colonel insignia on his collar was the only military dress he wore. His clothes were civilian work coveralls and comfortable slip-on shoes. His short hair was graying at the temples. His middle age was showing.

The transport ship's command deck was an open floor divided into five sections, each with its own set of work stations. The shift commander, sitting in the central command chair, acknowledged Danny's arrival with a nod before turning back to his duties.

Over in the communications area, Lieutenant Reynolds was talking with the comm officer. He excused himself and joined Danny.

"Good morning, Colonel."

"Lieutenant. How do things look?"

"We're two days from Station Hilo," said Reynolds.

"No problems then?"

"Eight years of quiet," said Reynolds. This had been Danny's second stretch in cryo since departing the Takiree quadrant. "We'll drop your team off at ten hundred hours day after tomorrow. Hilo has a shuttle to take you on to Old Earth System."

"Thank you," Danny said calmly. "That's good news."

Lieutenant Reynolds hesitated, finally asked curiously, "Old Earth, sir?"

Danny gave the man a pat on the arm before turning back to the exit. "I'm hoping for a family reunion, Lieutenant."

Claire and Amelia walked the well-traveled trail through tangles of thick brush and scrubby-looking trees. The trail wound its way around and through dozens of rusting hulks of long-abandoned spacecraft, brought there and left to die hundreds of years ago, the ships overgrown now by vines and bramble.

Claire led the way, occasionally using her wooden staff to push aside a thorny vine or blackberry bush that threatened to swallow the trail.

The sisters stepped into a large clearing that was encircled by a high perimeter wall of trees and brush. Their shuttle was there, taking up the entire north end of the clearing, the hull half hidden by the encroaching vegetation. Also in the clearing was a small storage shed, a smoke house, a large vegetable garden, a picnic table and a barbeque pit.

Claire took Amelia's backpack from her sister and walked over to a heavy work bench. She set their gear on the counter and began sorting through it as Amelia went into the shuttle.

The shuttle used the bare minimum of power. They kept proximity sensors operating, but brought up other systems only as needed. Amelia interfaced with systems on Station Delta once weekly. Should anyone attempt to make contact with them it would likely be by way of the space station. As importantly, the station also monitored inner-solar system activity and they would like to know if anyone was in the neighborhood.

Amelia turned on the emergency overhead lighting as she entered the main compartment. This provided enough light for most of their tasks. There was additional lighting available to them whenever they needed it.

They had brought the shuttle down to the planet's surface three years earlier, this after spending more than twenty six years on the station, the majority of that time in cryo. By Amelia's most recent calculations, at current power usage the shuttle would go completely dark in another eleven months. She didn't like the idea of losing contact with the station, but didn't see any way around it.

And they had long ago lost the ability to lift off the surface. They were planet-side for good.

Once the shuttle could no longer communicate with the station, there would be little reason to stay with it. Claire was already making plans to move. She wanted to build a cabin, a barn, and start a farm proper. She had her sights set on a piece of land bordering a river some three days travel to the south.

Amelia certainly wouldn't mind the additional living space, but there were issues with Claire's plans, most significantly for the very reason they had chosen not to establish a more visible presence right where they were.

But... circumstances change. Who knew what those circumstances might be in another year?

Claire came into the shuttle just as Amelia returned to the main cabin after cleaning up. They passed each other as Claire took her turn aft to shower and change, Amelia settling into the chair at the computer station. She activated the computer, brought up the comm system and established the connection with Delta Station. She spent the next few minutes going through the station's previous week's logs.

She was shutting down the connection when Claire came back into the main cabin.

"Any news?" asked Claire, pulling her hair back into a pony tail. She was dressed now in clean clothes.

"No one called to say hi," she said. "But it looks like we have company."

Claire sat on the edge of the table, pulled her feet up onto the chair. "The Takiree are back..."

"They're in the neighborhood; well inside Mars orbit."

The Takiree had made it through the Labyrinth a year after Claire and Amelia had moved from the station and down to Old Earth. The sisters had hunkered down and played dead for weeks while the Takiree searched the planet for signs of human activity. Since then they dropped in now and again, usually only making cursory searches.

"All right. We'll have to go dark," said Claire. They didn't know what sensors the Takiree used, so in the past turned off all tech and kept out of sight during the periodic visits. The shuttle itself was well camouflaged, just one more ship in the graveyard; and it was hoped that if the Takiree used heat sensors that their individual body heat revealed them to be just two more animals amongst the abundant wildlife.

"There's not much left for us to turn off," said Amelia. "We're already about as dark as we can get."

They did have the proximity sensors, but usually kept them active. Most everything else was shut down. Amelia wouldn't be connecting with the space station now for another week.

Claire frowned. "Yeah, we are rather off the grid, aren't we?"

The first signs of dawn were creeping into the main cabin from the open airlock in the next compartment; a soft gray slowly pushed its way in, moved across the floor and well into the room. A cool breeze drifted in, and there was a hint of morning dew in the air.

Amelia and Claire were asleep in their bunks, formally their cryo tubes. Claire slept in the upper bunk, her sister in the lower.

An amber light began to pulse: slowly, steadily. It sent a golden glow throughout the cabin. After half a dozen seconds, the pulsating light was accompanied by a rhythmic attention signal, the alarm just loud enough to bring the sisters out of their slumber.

Both managed to maintain a sense of calm as they climbed out of bed. Both dressed quickly, Amelia as she moved to the monitors. She shut off the alarms.

Claire was standing just inside the open hatch. She looked back at her sister. "Waddya see, Amelia?"

"Still a couple of miles north, coming this way, slow." She shut down the sensors. "I think it's a pair of drones."

"All right," said Claire. "You ready?"

Amelia was already turning and standing. They stepped out of the shuttle together and hurried across the clearing to the supply shed. Claire brought out a pair of light daypacks, already prepped with emergency provisions. They left the clearing and quickly worked their way to a preplanned location in the brush a few hundred yards north.

As they didn't know what sensors the drones might have, they long ago decided it best not to draw attention to their home base. They also felt that if the drones were in fact equipped with heat sensors, best they be seen as a pair of animals in the brush rather than a couple of bodies in one of the supposedly abandoned craft in the spaceship graveyard.

They settled in beside the trunk of a great tree with a wide canopy spread above, creating a small clearing beneath it surrounded by brush; they waited, watching the dawn sky peeking through branches and leaves.

A minute later came the muted hum of Takiree craft. Claire cocked her head sideways, took in the sound. She looked then to Amelia, held up two fingers and nodded.

Amelia had been right: Drones; two of them.

The craft were upon them a few moments later. One passed several hundred feet to their left, the other some distance to their right. They caught only a quick glimpse of the nearer. Three meters long, cylindrical, a pair of wings near the bow and smaller stabilizer wings aft.

And then they were past. It took another half minute for the sound to fade and the early morning quiet to return.

Claire shifted about on her heels, leaned against the tree trunk and slid down to a sitting position.

"So," she said, just managing to mask her sense of relief. "What's for breakfast?"

A long-dead city lay an easy one day's march north of the spaceship graveyard. Claire and Amelia came to the abandoned town every three or four weeks. They often took the time on these outings to explore the ruins, looking for stuff they might be able to use, and they often spent a night or two camped in the protection of broken concrete walls, but their stated reason for being there was the good hunting that lay just beyond the city.

They walked side-by-side down the wide, rubble-strewn boulevard that would take the sisters through the heart of the downtown. None of the buildings had survived the centuries of neglect. Iron framework skeletons of buildings with hanging broken chunks of wall lined the streets; great shards of concrete rose dozens of feet from the remains building foundations.

Claire slowed, listening, turning her head to one side and then the other. She appeared to be stretching her senses far beyond this street. She stopped then, holding her staff to one side.

Amelia took another few steps before stopping and looking back to her sister.

"What is it?" she asked.

"I hear something," said Claire.

Amelia listened, tried to hear what her sister was hearing. There was only the sound of the gentle breeze whispering through the broken walls of the nearest buildings.

"Nothing," she said.

"Listen," Claire said, almost a hush. "Listen."

She listened. And then... very faint. Very distant.

There, thought Amelia. *Yes...*

"An engine?" she asked.

Claire turned her gaze to Amelia.

"I think it's—" She looked up, outward... south. She couldn't see anything. "It's coming this way."

Amelia indicated the concrete remnants of one corner of the nearest building. They moved quickly over, clambered into the rubble and squatted down in the shadows. They sat in silence, struggled to hear the incoming threat. It took another few seconds before the sound was clear, distinct.

Something was definitely out there, and it was coming nearer.

"It's not a drone," said Amelia.

It didn't have the soft hum of a Takiree drone.

"No," said Claire. "Not a drone."

Moments later the sound was directly above them and rushing past. The Takiree ship was visible for only a couple of seconds. It was maybe a hundred feet above them and appeared to be descending.

"Come on," said Claire. She was up and scrambling out of the shadows.

"Claire!" Amelia whispered harshly, as if the Takiree might hear her.

Claire wasn't hanging around to argue the matter. She was hurrying up the street, heading in the direction of the descending alien craft.

Eight blocks up, the boulevard circled a city park, mostly overgrown now. In the center of the park was an open plaza. The Takiree shuttlecraft had landed on the plaza. The alien craft was smaller than Claire and Amelia's shuttle, closer in size to the small jumpers that Claire had first trained in so long ago.

By the time the sisters reached the park, hiding behind the thick bramble of blackberry that had overtaken the south side of the park, they only just caught a glimpse of two figures stepping back into the ship.

Claire and Amelia had never seen a Takiree before. All they saw now were two shadowy silhouettes disappearing into the shadows in their tiny craft. They appeared slightly shorter than an average human, thin bodies and long arms.

"Feldafarb," grumbled Claire.

"Really?" asked Amelia. "They could have seen us, Claire. They still might."

"I was hoping to see what they looked like."

"One head, two arms, two legs. Can we go now?"

Claire wasn't ready to leave. She studied the park surrounding the plaza and the alien craft. "What are they doing here?"

"I don't know." Amelia had wondered that herself, but she wasn't so curious as to want to hang around. "Maybe they're checking on something one of their drones saw."

Claire frowned at that idea. There wasn't much around that should draw the interest of the Takiree. What might a drone have seen that would bring them all the way out here?

And that begged the question... where was this Takiree craft based?

Amelia shifted position, caught her sleeve on the bush they were using as cover.

"Maybe they like blackberries."

One of the Takiree appeared again in the open hatch of their small shuttle. It stepped down and away from the ship. They were too far away to see its face or features, but they could see that it was dressed in loose-fitting pants and jacket, perhaps military; a uniform of some kind, at the very least.

It turned and looked back to the ship. The hatch closed, and a moment later the shuttle lifted off. It rose about fifty feet before smoothly gliding away, continuing to rise at it did.

The individual that had been left behind started across the park, away from Claire and Amelia.

"Is it going on an explore?" Claire wondered aloud, though in a low whisper.

"Hey, you're not thinking of—"

"No, no, no," Claire said quickly. She rose up from her crouch and started to back away. "Let's get the heck out of here."

Claire settled onto her familiar spot on the corner of the table, propped her feet up on the chair as she watched Amelia take a seat at the computer station.

They had been laying low for three days. There had been no sign of the Takiree anywhere in the area since the landing in the dead city. Whatever the bad guys had been up to, it hadn't brought them to the graveyard.

Amelia activated the proximity sensors that had been shut down these past days. They waited expectantly.

No pulsing alert light, no alarm.

"Well, that's a good sign," sighed Claire.

Amelia studied the monitors. "There's nothing in the air."

"Right. And so?" she urged, waving a hand at the computer.

"Yeah, okay..." Amelia said cautiously. She brought up the main computer, activated the comm with Delta Station. It took her another half minute to interface with the space station's systems.

Incoming data showed the station sensors had last tracked an alien cruiser in the inner solar system two days previous. It also noted the earth orbit presence of two alien shuttlecraft several times during the week prior to that.

All appeared clear at the moment, though they couldn't know for certain that there wasn't a presence planet-side, but beyond the range of the proximity sensors, nor whether any bad guys had been left on the ground anywhere on the planet. After all, there was that one alien they had seen walking away from the alien shuttle.

But it hadn't been looking for them. If it had, it wouldn't have been alone.

And one wandering alien certainly wasn't an invasion.

"Hey, Sis..." Amelia said slowly, staring at the monitor.

"What is it?" Claire was suddenly anxious.

"A message."

Claire slid off the table and stood behind Amelia.

Amelia had her eyes focused on the monitor. "No indication as to how it got there, but there's a message saved in the comm logs; several days old." She went silent as she continued to study the data splashed on the screen. Claire waited.

"Coded," said Amelia. She worked at the keys for a few seconds. "It's from Danny."

"After all these years..."

"Text only." Amelia read then: "Approaching Labyrinth. Seeking family."

"That's it?"

"Isn't that enough?"

Claire thought about that. She looked away, looked aft to the next compartment, to the daylight streaming in through the open hatch.

Amelia looked up at Claire.

"Are you all right?"

"Yeah," said Claire. "I think I'll go for a walk."

Amelia watched her sister leave the main cabin, then turned back to the computer. She disengaged from Delta Station and shut down the system, leaving the proximity sensors active.

Stepping down out of the shuttle, she found Claire over in the vegetable garden. The mid-morning sun wasn't yet above the perimeter trees, so that entire section of the clearing was still in the shade.

She walked up to the edge of the garden. Claire was on her knees midway along one row. It looked like she was pulling weeds.

"I thought you were going for a walk."

"Started to," she said absently. "Saw some weeds, then saw some more."

Amelia glanced around the clearing, looked back again to her sister.

"Claire. Really, are you all right?"

"I'm fine." She continued weeding. She hesitated then, stared at a clump of weed in her hand. The root was broken. The weed would be growing back.

She sat back on her heels, finally looked up at Amelia.

"Amelia... do you ever think about Mom and Dad?"

"Sure. They creep into my thoughts almost every day."

"Me too." Claire sighed, tossed the weeds out beyond the garden bed. "Mom, Dad, Uncle Marcus. All these years, we've only had Danny. And he came to us second hand; just an image on a monitor or a cryptic text message stored in a log."

"And now..."

"Yes. And now."

What news might Danny bring?

"Claire, are you worried?"

Claire looked away from her sister. "We never knew. You know, what happened. Not for sure. Danny never said anything. He and Uncle Marcus transferred our canisters into that shuttle. That's all we know. That's all we ever really knew for sure."

Neither said anything for several moments. Claire rose up then, brushed dirt from her hands.

"Do you ever think about that?"

"I do. All the time."

Claire looked about the clearing, not really seeing anything. "Yeah. Not like we could ask, right?"

"We'll know soon enough, Claire," said Amelia. "Sis... whatever happened, it happened two hundred years ago."

Claire looked directly at Amelia, started to respond to that, to tell Amelia that it hadn't been two hundred years for them. For them it was closer to seven years. But Amelia knew that. And she knew that Amelia was feeling exactly what she was feeling.

She stepped out of the garden bed and started away. "I'm going to take that walk now."

Marcus Bradford worked his way from the command deck down to the airlock, eager to greet the newest arrival. He had been on Delta Station for only four days, knew that his nephew's shuttle hadn't been far behind, negotiating its way through the Labyrinth.

Marcus had made three trips to the far side of the galaxy over the years, most of that time spent in cryo; this while Danny had lived half his life. They had worked together for almost a year following that day when they had placed Claire and Amelia into the shuttle and sent it on its way, but since that time had crossed paths only twice in the two centuries that had passed since.

So the uncle was now a bit younger than the nephew, though he too was starting to gray around the temples.

Danny and two of his team were already through the airlock and into the station by the time Marcus reached them. He stopped in the passageway, welcomed the new arrivals and allowed Danny's companions to pass, directing them to the station mess.

He stepped up to Danny, then. "So it's *Colonel*, now," he said. He reached out to Danny and gave him a hug.

Danny mumbled something about retiring soon if they let him, and then they followed after the others down the passage. They exchanged a few minor pleasantries en route to the mess, and then Danny asked about conditions on the station.

It was empty but for Marcus and his small team. They would have their pick of quarters, and the galley was still well supplied.

"And what about the Takiree?" asked Danny. There had been no sign of them outside the Labyrinth perimeter, nor as they had traversed the Labyrinth to the station.

According to station's logs, all had been quiet for several weeks. Prior to that, the Takiree had been buzzing about Old Earth like flies for almost a month; cruisers, a number of drones. But they were long gone by the time Marcus arrived.

They both knew the Takiree had been significantly weakened over the past years, and hoped the Jaung could finally defeat them. They had to wonder why the Takiree bothered with Old Earth at all. Perhaps they weren't looking for humans in hiding. Maybe they were looking for a hideaway of their own.

Danny sat at one of the tables in the mess, cup of coffee in hand. His companions were at a table nearby. Marcus settled into the chair opposite. He waited, and when Danny didn't say anything, decided to bring up the subject himself.

"They were here," he stated.

Danny rubbed at his face, the tension in his body appearing to dissolve.

"Oh, boy..." he managed.

"We found a message saved in the comm log; not much, listed their arrival date, departure date. They were here for twenty six years; a lot of that time in cryo."

"How long ago did they leave?"

"About three years ago."

Danny stared down at his coffee again. He took a drink, swallowed. "All these years, I never knew if they ever saw even one of my messages. Or if they were even alive."

"Well... they were alive up to three years ago. They were here, and it was you that brought 'em."

The cryptic messages, the supply pod, the even more cryptic directions and half-completed code sequences. And through all of it, Danny had to have considered and planned for circumstances that were decades out, never knowing the way of things in the future.

"Do you suppose they're on Old Earth?" Danny asked. He hadn't actually directed them there, but he had guided not so subtly, and hoped. But so much had depended on the circumstances that existed when and if they arrived at Delta Station.

Wherever they went, they hadn't gone straight away. Marcus had said they had remained at the station, going into cryo, so they hadn't been ready then. It was more than a quarter of a century before they decided to move on.

But to where? Had they gone to Old Earth?

"We're headin' that way in any case," said Marcus. "What say we find out?" He gave a wink, took another sip of his coffee.

Amelia came out of the shuttle and walked calmly over to the supply shed. She brought out two backpacks and two pair of hiking boots. She was half finished packing before Claire came out of the smoke house.

Amelia gave her an affirmative nod, tossed Claire's boots in her direction and continued packing. Claire took the boots over to the picnic table and changed out of her shoes. Five minutes later they were away from the clearing, following an obscure trail leading east.

Amelia's weekly uplink to Delta Station had brought news. The station's tracking had identified several recent traverses through the Labyrinth, one of which had to have been Danny. Both craft had been identified as of human design. Both had docked at Delta Station.

And then Amelia located an encoded message recently left in the logs. It had been Danny. He noted his arrival at the station, as well as that of Uncle Marcus a few days earlier. They acknowledged reading the brief message left behind by the sisters.

A second message, more cryptic than the first, appeared to contain coordinates. If correct, the location was two days hike to the east; practically in the neighborhood.

They travelled till almost dusk, when they reached a semi-permanent campsite of theirs. It was now partially overgrown, as they hadn't come this way in almost a year. They cleared away the encroaching brush, cleaned up the fire pit and finished setting up camp.

Sitting before the small campfire after dinner, Claire brought up what they had both been thinking about since calculating the coordinates they have been given.

"If they knew we were here, they wouldn't have landed two days away. They would have landed in the next clearing."

"Danny did say he was seeking family," said Amelia.

"He left that message before he entered the Labyrinth," said Claire. "They don't even know we're on the planet."

"I expect that's true," said Amelia. "But they hope we're here. After all, Danny directed us here."

Danny had actually only directed them as far as Delta Station, but they assumed he had wanted them to choose Old Earth over attempting to navigate out of the Labyrinth and going somewhere else, possibly home. He just couldn't openly tell them to go planet-side.

But the coordinates they had decrypted were only two days march from them. An entire planet, and Danny lands only two days away?

That's what was really bugging Claire. Forty miles away had to be more than a coincidence, but it wasn't about his sisters. It wasn't about them.

What would bring them to those coordinates, and how had Claire and Amelia ended up planting roots so near?

Was it the spaceship graveyard? The graveyard had served them well as a nice hiding place for their little shuttle. Might it also serve as a marker of some kind? For what?

Claire sat quietly then, watching the flames of their little fire, looking deeply into the glowing coals beneath.

So there was something else nearby.

The sisters broke camp the next morning well before dawn, the world around them just light enough to travel by. An hour after sunrise they were following what had at one time been a major highway, was now little more than a wide, smooth band of yellow grass stretching out nearly to the horizon. They occasionally came across large, metal panels lying on the ground, the paint on the fallen road signs having long since faded away.

Late afternoon... they approached the outer perimeter of the remnants of a small county airport. The hangars, service buildings and tower were gone, leaving only the open expanse, a few piles of rotted wood and bent sheet metal. There was a shuttle not much larger than their own parked midway along the vestiges of what had once been the concrete airstrip. There were several figures moving about near the shuttle, and several others rummaging about one of the piles of wood and metal a hundred yards from the shuttle.

Claire and Amelia watched from the shadows of the treeline.

"What do you think?" asked Amelia. From this distance, the figures looked human.

"It must be them," said Claire. "Who else would it be?"

Amelia spoke quite matter-of-factly: "Then why are we still hiding here in the trees?"

Claire studied the scene a few moments more, finally let out a loud sigh and straightened.

"Right. Let's go."

They stepped out of the trees and started across the grassy field bordering the long-abandoned airfield. They were nearly halfway to the shuttle before two of the figures stepped away and started toward them.

Danny looked to be well into his fifties, Uncle Marcus a few years younger.

"Aren't you a welcome sight," said Danny, still six or seven paces away.

"We were in the neighborhood," said Claire. *Literally...*

The four exchanged hugs and tearful welcomes. They talked over each other as each tried to get a word in about cryptic messages and empty planets and years in cryo and gray hair.

They grew unexpectedly silent, looked at one another with broad, inane smiles. They suddenly reached out and hugged each other all over again.

Once they managed to pull apart yet again, Claire asked how they had found them here.

Danny shook his head. "We weren't sure you were here at all. I tried to be optimistic, but..."

One of the people who had been digging into the massive pile of debris approached the reunion.

"Sorry to disturb you, Colonel," he said, turning then to Marcus. "Marcus. The way is clear."

"Thanks, Jack," said Marcus. "We're right behind you."

The group followed Jack, continuing their conversation as they walked.

Danny had hoped that Claire and Amelia had chosen to come to Old Earth, and that they would choose to settle in the spaceship graveyard, use it as cover. But he could never let on the importance of this location. The Takiree had to believe that whatever the original importance of Old Earth, that it had been abandoned, as the evidence provided suggested.

Claire smirked. "You mean in the same way you led <u>us</u> here and then abandoned us?"

"It worked, eh?"

Claire smirked again, but she had to give him that. It had worked.

Amelia agreed. But...

"What is it that's so important?" she asked.

"Shall we see?" asked Marcus. They reached the pile of rubble. Much of it had been pulled aside, exposing a large metal door. Those who had cleared the way now stepped aside. Marcus reached down and slid aside an iron bar, then pulled the door open.

It exposed an access shaft four feet across leading down into the dark. Cool air rose up from deep below.

The last time Marcus had been here, two centuries earlier, they had used a freight elevator a hundred yards away. That had been sealed off, leaving only this shaft to get back inside.

"I'm afraid it's all ladder for the trip down," he said. "And dark. We won't have power until we get below."

Marcus started down.

Danny gave his sisters a grin and a wink, then climbed onto the ladder. Claire followed, and then Amelia. The others remained topside, starting back to the shuttle once Amelia began her descent. There were other tasks above ground yet to be completed.

The opening above Amelia grew smaller and dim, until finally it was little more than a speck of light, the shaft an all-consuming black. The only sounds were those of hands and feet on the ladder rungs and the breathing of the four climbers.

More than a minute later Amelia heard a different sound drifting up from below; the faint hum of support systems.

She stepped from the ladder just as Marcus pulled down a lever, bringing a diffused glow to the cavern.

Amelia had expected a cavern, but had thought it would be more, would be something larger. This cavern was smaller than she expected. It was fifty feet wide, no more than two hundred feet deep. It was forty feet from floor to ceiling, and the platform they were standing on was about twenty feet above the floor.

On the floor were eight rows of cryo canisters, starting directly below them and running to the far end. Amelia estimated about a hundred and sixty sleepers in all.

Danny looked thoughtfully out across the rows of cryo tubes.

"Those first weeks, first months really, we didn't know what was happening. We stayed with the transport cruiser at first, did what we could to protect those in cryo. Many sections of the ship had been damaged; entire compartments destroyed, like the one you two had been in."

But when it became clear what was going on, they knew they had to get as many as they could to safety. But just bringing them out of cryo wasn't going to be enough. They knew they had to protect them for the time after... to rebuild.

"The future would need people like your parents," said Marcus.

Their mother had been a ranking member of the Council of Governors. Their father was a planetary scientist with extensive experience in all the disciplines. Both parents would be desperately needed once the conflict was over, however it ended.

And so Danny joined the fight against the Takiree while Marcus set about to create doomsday vaults like this one. Dozens just like this, containing the seeds of humanity, scattered about on dozens of worlds...

Dozens of tiny human colonies to rise from the ashes should things go really bad; insurance that the human race wouldn't go extinct.

The four grew silent. For a few moments there was only the faint hum of the support systems caring for the sleepers.

Amelia turned then and looked expectantly at Marcus. Marcus sensed the focus, looked side-glance at his niece and then nodded out to the floor.

"First row. Canisters four and five."

Amelia was sitting at her computer station on the command deck in Delta Station. She was working second shift, monitoring the Labyrinth defense systems. A four-ship squadron had been traversing the Labyrinth for almost three weeks and was now approaching the station.

She continued to monitor, though Control had the job of actually guiding them in.

Claire was in one of those ships, returning from patrol.

There had been no sign of the Takiree within the Labyrinth perimeter for some time, but there were still a number of enemy cruisers in this sector, and more beyond. Humans crossed swords with them from time to time, but the weakened Takiree were more concerned with the Jaung these days. Trying to conscript another race to do their dirty work hadn't gone so well the last time and they weren't all that eager to attempt it again.

Amelia finished her shift about half an hour after Claire docked and cleared security. She met her coming out of the locker room.

"Hey, Sis," said Claire. They continued down the hall. "Wanna head over to the rec room? I just have to stop by my quarters."

"Shouldn't you be getting some rest?"

"I got plenty of rest trudging through the Labyrinth. I need some activity."

They turned into the main passageway and approached the quarters sector.

"Sure," said Amelia. "I'll just keep you company."

They turned down a side passage and stopped outside Claire's quarters. Claire pressed her palm on the reader and the door slid aside. Amelia followed Claire into the room.

Claire disappeared through a side door, Amelia walked over to the porthole. Old Earth was visible, a large blue, green and white ball set against the black of space several hundred thousand miles distant.

"Are you ready for our trip planet-side?" she called out. "We're leaving tomorrow, you know."

"No problem; plenty of time," said Claire from the other room. "Ten minutes to pack, and I'm set."

The colony of a hundred and sixty had grown considerably. Hundreds of immigrants had arrived over the past year. Several thousand more were en route.

Claire and Amelia had been there at the beginning, when the sleepers were awakened; had been there to welcome their parents, to guide them through those first confusing days. They had stayed then to help their parents establish the community.

But there had also been a demand for personnel on the reawakened Delta Station and the Labyrinth defense network, a demand for skills that Claire and Amelia possessed.

Claire came back into the room and stood beside her sister. She was dressed for a martial arts workout, something she had picked up since moving back to Delta Station.

She looked out at the view.

"It'll be nice seeing Mom and Dad," she said. "Two weeks seems a bit much, though."

"Planet-side isn't so bad," said Amelia, to herself as much as to Claire. *And family is important.*

"Uh, huh," sighed Claire, rather half-heartedly. "Any word from Danny?"

"They can't make it."

"Hmm. Too bad."

Danny and Marcus were helping coordinate the establishment of the fledgling federation of colonies. Old Earth had been made the headquarters for the federation, but there was as yet very little in the way of a coalition. For now it was a title only.

Claire and Amelia's mother was to be the first head of Council, once there was one.

The upcoming visit had nothing to do with any of that. This was strictly family.

"It wouldn't take much, you know..." said Claire.

"What's that?"

"To make her spaceworthy."

It took a moment. Amelia smiled wistfully.

Their little shuttle was still in the graveyard. Bringing it back to life would take a lot of work, and considerable refitting. And it would need a new power core.

Still. It was just waiting there, right where they left it...

Claire let out another long sigh.

"I miss it," she said softly. *Out there...*

"I know," said Amelia.

Claire stared coolly at Old Earth. She gave her sister a slight nudge. "We could just head the other way."

"Yeah," Amelia mumbled under her breath. *That would be nice...*

"So?"

"No... No, we couldn't." *Duties, responsibilities...*

Claire and Amelia stared out through the porthole, into space, into the black that lay beyond the planet in the distance.

"You sure?" asked Claire.

~ end

Printed in Great Britain
by Amazon

47267547R00078